The Wizard's Testament

An Unexpected Challenge

by Billy Ironcrane

For permissions contact:
www.ironcrane.com/html/contactus.html

Published by:
Mc Cabe and Associates, Tacoma, WA.

Illustrated by Renee Knarreborg
Cover Design Mc Cabe and Associates
Cover image by Doug Goodman "Crow"
Cover background - https://unsplash.com/@lucahuter

ISBN-13: 978-1-7324154-6-1
Library of Congress Control Number: 2021922664

To Bryan Smith
Whose generous spirit lifts others to their full potential.

To Master Isidro Archibeque
(5/12/1933 - 1/9/2021)
Teacher, friend and wellspring of endless inspiration.

Contents

Illustrations

The
Wizard's
Testament

Introduction

There once existed a great dynasty. It spanned nearly four centuries. Us? No - not quite. Long before our time. The people back then considered themselves blessed. Heaven's chosen. Quite like how we see ourselves. They knew they had stumbled into a golden era. Nothing in the long history of their land came remotely close. In marketplaces, abundance evident, everyday folk playfully bantered over how many times they had to be reborn to deserve this auspicious fate. A birth-rite of luck and good fortune favoring nearly all.

Common terms and phrases dubbed their empire "the world." Its very name meant "The Central State." Center of what? Why, center of everything of course! Flags and banners could be seen everywhere. They were proud, and proud of being proud. What else was there? Everybody looked to them and wanted what they had. So they thought. Sound familiar? These same propensities echo and resonate just about everywhere. Just flip through the pages of recorded history.

At their zenith, an immense sense of freedom and possibility pervaded their culture. It seemed anybody possessing connections and determination could do or be anything. Among them, some grew spectacularly affluent and powerful. The soaring influence of those fortunate few took on life of its own. In only a few generations, an empire of privilege and dominance manifested within the empire of flesh, toil and substance.

Leveraging chicanery and cunning manipulation the wealthy and dominant eventually assumed control. It started when they devised clever networks of extended influence. You couldn't even find their trails if you looked. Just the effects. Then they gained laws ensuring they'd keep whatever they gathered and could pass it down forever to their own. "Why not?" they reasoned. "Who deserves it more than us? Could any of it even exist without us?" Thus secured, their focus thereafter turned toward gleaning more from the many, first targeting the weak. Perhaps assumed control is too kind in portraying what they did.

Fittingly, their empire, like many others before and since, became just another imprint in the trail of history, left by the swinging pendulum of humankind's convoluted affairs. First one way, then the other. Inception, growth, arrival at full maturity, then a turning down to decline, decay and finish. Little more than dust remained when done. Just as when it started. Mingled with much blood of course. There is that price to be paid.

It's regrettable, though not rare by any stretch. What started and flourished under exemplary rule became corrupted. Expectations and hopes aside, disappointments became the norm among the many. At first, the changes were barely perceptible. They came on with the subtlety of a seasonal affliction. One could see it over there, but not here. Why worry? But then it spread. How like a canker. Chewing away from the inside, spewing rot from its tail. Growing as though to defy all imaginings, degrading all in its wake. Eventually the scale tipped and demanded a reckoning. To nearly everyone's disbelief, what once seemed solid and immutable disintegrated from within. Institutions of state and equity tottered and crumbled from their own corrupted and now unwieldy mass.

After the great fall, those left had their own way of summing it up, "Divided, must unite; united, must divide." Their philosophies and beliefs made clear how these eternal tendencies drove all things and propelled time into view from the void. What to take from it all? Simply this. Always look carefully to what goes on in your world. It's where you make a difference — our common birthright. That's what guides the characters in all our stories. Those who rely on stigma, ridicule, deception and domination have departed in their doing, from the great way. Abandoning compassion and betraying the common bond will leave chaos and want. Those shortfalls drive all empires to their end. Should that be where you finish, you won't be alone.

Background

Just as everything seemed destined for extinction, there arose what many deemed the last chance. Three great leaders emerged to contend for power.

First among their objectives, secure the divine right to revive the once empire. Each sought to renew and preserve the Mandate of Heaven. Establish legitimacy, and with that some semblance of continuity. On this crucial point they all failed, and had no choice but to make do without. Indeed, a pity. For nearly five generations, bedlam reigned. The once glorious empire fractured into three unendingly contentious warring kingdoms.

Stories from that era linger in the fabric of collective mythology. Like carefully preserved trails, their portrayals of sacrifice, loss, struggle, hope, heroism and achievement speak to our essential natures. Guideposts, worn by change. Fading at times from view, still they call out. Hinting to where we head and how we might end.

Though precise details may be elusive, we have the best efforts and records of early historians to light our path. The doings and achievements of the many heroes, along with the misdeeds of their villainous counterparts, have been elegantly preserved. Their many aspects and reflections shine forth from finely honed works[1] of artists, poets and writers. Who better to reveal reality, and what we should make of it?

We know one thing for certain. Culminating that tumultuous period, what remained came briefly under one rule. Then in a quick moment, like a precious vase carelessly mishandled, it shattered completely. From there, it reeled fragmented and hopeless for hundreds of years. A new blight of warlords re-delivered the population to disunity, carnage, starvation, disease, indenture and destitution.

Our current story begins there. A world where common people, good people, have no home and either sell out or become branded as outlaws or undesirables. Traitors and enemies. Join us as we scour through the remnants strewn about the landscape of time and events. Might they ever meld into a coherent whole? A vessel perhaps? One capable of lifting us from the failures of our predecessors and delivering a working portion of hope for the future.

Perhaps we are that portion? Who can say? As with the heroes in the story, it will be our future regardless. Will we be worthy of their example? Should we too consider ourselves blessed?

---

[1] There are a number of commendable resources available. Among my favorites is: Luo, Guanzhong, and Moss Roberts. *Three Kingdoms: a Historical Novel; Complete and Unabridged.* Berkeley: Univ. of California Press, 2005. Print.

First Awakening

Listening intently, the dragon
hears the nightingale's song, the cricket's crick
A grasshopper's hop, weaving through brush thick
Swift's wings clutching wisps of air
Whispers of freedom everywhere

Eyes half closed, and root held tight
How shines this mirror dustless and right
Through listening eyes, the dragon clears the night.

Middle Kingdom

Northern Tribes

Changcheng

Huang He

Western Wilderness

Wei He

Wei

Huang He

Yellow Sea

Jing Territory Midlands

Shu

Crystal Springs

Yangzi Jiang

Fortune's Gateway

Ling Village

Yangzi Jiang

Eastern Sea

Warlord States

Southern Mountains

Southlands

Guangdong

Zhuya Commandry

Southern Sea

Pearl Cliffs

R.Knarreborg 2019

Empire Adrift

Part 1

Poets and Perils

Poets

The evening went peacefully. Worn, tired and cold from their long trek, the two warmed by the fire. Back then, storytelling at day's end was common. Passing time before succumbing to weariness, they recalled the exemplary lives and deeds of heroes past. Lives lived which brightly lit the trail for all fledgling steps toward righteousness. Then they slept. Such reminiscences ofttimes reach far into our dreams - before becoming part of our being.

A sound in the far distance pulled Bao Ling from his rest. He listened intently. *Just the woods talking,* he concluded. As light broke from the east, he still lay listening, as had become his way. For one like Bao Ling, survival depended on hearing everything. His ears had long been attuned to all directions. On this particular day, he heard only the expected morning sounds. Eyes now open, he measured the slow drift of the White Star above. Said to govern metal, instruments of combat, and the affairs of war, the planet seemed to move opposite its normal path. He knew from the folklore of his people, such retrograde motion signaled unsure turns and disturbances, particularly in the affairs of men.

As Bao Ling's eyes half closed to anxious thoughts of what next, Zhi Mei rose and skirted about to make morning fire. Her voice spun tunes rising atop those of the early birds. All in unison calling greeting to the coming day.

Brothers in a Peach Garden
Dancing with destiny
A sandal maker
A curd vendor
A butcher
Sworn brothers three[2]

Three apart from the world's dust
Shining stars for all to see
Together in righteous quests
For all eternity

A mind, a heart, and a body strong
Bring peace, restore hope, their toils long
Enter Zhuge Liang, soul of dragon stolen from his sleep
Brothers now four, struggles now steep

King Liu, above all to keep
A clear eye before the leap
Take not more than fate has given
Lest all dreams to dust are driven

---

[2] Referring to the Peach Garden Oath. Liu Bei, Guan Yu and Zhang Fei - three friends of new acquaintance. They swear an oath of loyalty and brotherhood dedicating their lives and destinies to serving the people and restoring the empire. Together they declare their unison until death, hoping only that when it comes, it takes them together.

Bao Ling listened intently as the verses unfolded. Each layered upon the last. How delicately Zhi Mei set the balance of righteousness against the winds of fate and time — a rabbit dashing blindly in the brush as the lynx and hawk scoured the perimeter.

He feigned sleep, choosing to listen rather than arise and interrupt. He admired as Zhi Mei wound tales from the previous evening around all possible outcomes, finally ending with an old man, alone, wondering if righteousness were enough for a troubled life such as his. Bao Ling grappled with the thought, *Was I supposed to be that old man?*

"How can you do that?", he finally asked.

"It's just what I do. It's who I am."

"Yes, but how?"

"I never think about how. I just do it. My brother and father lived for their songs and poems, as do I. Father knew life's secrets were often obscured by the ordinary. He taught us how it was possible to lift the veil from those secrets, and to set them out for all to see and ponder. To that end, we would spend evenings singing, reciting, studying and challenging one another. I remember it as great fun. Sometimes, with diligence, I found my own meager efforts could push them to even greater insights. While others sought wealth, we sought harmony. Rather than gold, silver or jade, father's most precious possessions were his collections. They took a lifetime to gather, but he had

secured the Book of Songs, the Songs of Chu, the Music
Bureau Poems from the Han collections, even the works of
the Three Caos."

Bao Ling interrupted, "The Three Caos?"

"Yes," she replied, "Cao Cao, and his two sons Cao Pi
and Cao Zhi."

"You knew them as poets?", he asked, his surprise
evident.

She looked to Bao Ling, "Yes, great poets. It's likely I
know more of their poetry than I do of their supposed
exploits. For me, their poetry has always been real, a part of
my life. I've also heard tell of their deeds, and I know what
others have said. I judge them on their hearts and what I
know of their hearts from their words. Still, like everyone,
they were of the times, and doubtless, less than perfect. Of
the three, I recall how my father and brother tended most to
favor Cao Cao. You know him as the warlord king who
founded Wei. Then succeeded by son Cao Pi who in turn
forced the captive Emperor Xian to abdicate, thus sealing the
demise of Han.

"I inclined otherwise, preferring to favor Cao Zhi,
younger brother to Cao Pi. Vulnerable, human, honest. He
roamed the land, effectively barred for life from all power or
influence by his older brother."

Bao Ling answered, "Blood brothers at odds. How
unlike the history of the three brothers sworn."

Zhi Mei continued, "Yes, their relationship first bent awry when they competed to replace the deceased father. Cao Pi, ever politically astute, won handily, then relegated his brother to obscurity. Cao Zhi roamed about, often drunk, conjuring exquisite verses in the moment. Even in his delirium, his probing intellect ripped truth from the soul of his despair. But just as with many others, that 'itch' kept surfacing. It needed scratching. He wanted to serve and to gain distinction in propelling his father's ghostly ambitions forward. As you know, those same ambitions tilt and bob our fates even to this day. He forever looked to the court for opportunity to restore his rightful prominence as second son to Cao Cao.

"These efforts of course threatened elder brother Cao Pi, who succumbed to the ceaseless biddings of his counselors. 'You must once and for all eliminate Cao Zhi!' they cried. 'Your younger brother's very existence promises threat. His obvious talents will make him a magnet for rebels, renegades and malcontents.'

"So, they said! In the end, Cao Pi agreed, albeit reluctantly. He summoned his brother to imperial session. Being a sporting man, not unlike his father, Cao Pi granted one opportunity for the brother to save his own skin. Cao Pi looked to a painting, then ordered Cao Zhi to compose a poem. He must address all themes portrayed, without referring to any of the elements. Cao Zhi was to start walking, and to present the completed poem before the eighth step."

A Poem in Eight Steps

"Impossible!" cried Bao Ling. "Ignorant though I be, I know the degree of craft such a challenge demands."

"I agree. I could not have met the challenge — not so for the agile Cao Zhi. The counselors were stunned at his brilliant composition and the seemingly effortless assimilation of the multiple themes. Cao Pi, arguably his equal as a poet, recognized the accomplishment instantly. He said nothing. Then inexplicably, he summarily dismissed the effort as worthless. He turned to his brother and spoke 'While not satisfactory, your effort has at least earned you another attempt. Try again to convince me of your right to remain among us. Compose another. Now, on the spot! Use it to give full purview to the conundrum surrounding our fraternal brotherhood. You must do this without referring to either of us in any recognizable way.'

The counselors marveled at this challenge and whispered among themselves — 'A riddle without a solution.' Instantly, Cao Zhi approached his brother and delivered his verse. It took the form of a mournful song. A melody of deep despair and lost hope. He told of two beans from a common stalk. Now tossing about in a pot of boiling water, heated on a fire kindled by beanstalks. Together they wailed despondently over their common roots as each looked to supplant the other. Blinded by the boiling chaos which surrounded and threatened them both — while their roots and heritage disintegrated in flames below. Even their own ends stood certain."

"What then?" Bao Ling pressed on.

"All were silent and looked to Cao Pi, expecting to witness a deserved execution on the spot. Their thoughts, *The poem is an outrage, an insult!* Cao Pi stared his brother coldly in the eyes. He might have pulled his sword and taken Cao Zhi's head. We know he inherited his father's inclination toward explosive cruelty. Particularly when it became necessary to make a point. Perhaps for a fleeting moment the depraved sentiment winged through his thoughts. But for this once, restraint stayed his hand. The coldness in his eyes melted as the poet's words pushed through the ice. They conjured memories of early life together. Two brothers, under a loving and guiding father, who demanded, expected, and received loyalty, and deemed family to be life's greatest gift.

"Teardrops dripped to his royal tunic. Cao Pi immediately revoked the death sentence. In quick turn he ordered the counselors who argued for it to be beheaded, along with their families, allies and followers. He turned to all present and declared the issue settled for eternity. Henceforth anyone who recommended the death of his brother would be silenced with the same fate first, along with their families. He turned to his brother and affirmed his eternal love.

"Still, ever the practical man, he then stripped Cao Zhi of all titles, and barred him permanently from court. He then took extraordinary care his younger brother be well provided for. Secured for the balance of his days, which fortunately for us, were spent studying the flow of life's truths, and preserving them for all to experience through his crafted thoughts."

Bao Ling sat stonelike. Reminding of a Buddha in some lost wayside shrine, slight hints of a smile curled alongside his lips. Eyelids relaxed, his vision momentarily left the ordinary world and touched the plane of awareness.

"Bao Ling, are you all right?"

Hearing her words, his focus returned. He stared warmly into Zhi Mei's onyx eyes, smiling.

"I am in your debt."

"For what?" she asked.

"For bringing light to part of me that had become dark."

"No riddles, please," her inquisitive look made clear she expected more.

"You reminded me of something I once knew, but had completely forgotten. The stories of our people tell us of Cao Cao's ambition, and even his cruelty. Did he not spread plague to the Southland to weaken their defenses? Yet even in the midst of this unbridled ambition and his untold campaigns, he raised two extraordinary sons. Raised them as a loving parent would. Then imprinted them with his finest attributes as well as his base inclinations. In your account, I realized once again how powerless we are over how we are nurtured and the whims of fate — all constantly buffeted by winds of change. Just like the beans in the pot. Still, it is we who control how we see each other. What we do with that awareness becomes the actions which shape our karma.

"Cao Pi and Cao Zhi were no different than me — in their own way trying to reconnect with the way of life which matched their natures, nourished them, and brought them joy. It seems everyone has a Ling Village[3] disappearing behind them. They were constantly searching, hoping to somehow reconnect. Ultimately, they stood apart. Plagued by events which frustrated their aspirations. Still, even when paralyzed by distrust, and riddled by the insinuations of his counselors, Cao Pi could yet be stirred to reconnect with what for him had always been the essential truth. He loved his brother! That alone brought him out of his delirium. It was a last lifeline which, had he ignored, would have left him hollow, alone, and forever incomplete."

Zhi Mei pondered, then replied, "Perhaps you have come upon something to consider. But what do you make of what he does to his brother? And what of the counselors and their innocent families?"

---

[3] Specifics regarding the troubled history of Bao Ling's home can be found in our prior work, *Token Tales and Fragments.*

"This is my take, probably a false trail, but I'll offer it for what it is. At first, Cao Zhi stood ordained for death. Brother Cao Pi, coached to overflow in suspicion and distrust by his counselors, found in his brother's words a new perspective. From there, his own compassion's seed found new root, from which it sprung forth with conviction. All in a breath stealing instant! It returned the gift of life to Cao Zhi. Granted, a life of isolation and permanent detachment from the state founded by his father. For many, a fate equal to death. But for Cao Zhi, it would become the vehicle and inspiration for his art; as Cao Pi knew it would be."

Zhi Mei added, "Yes, but he died young, and his later works spoke of his despondency."

"Nothing is perfect, not even compassion. At least not so far as we in our limited way endeavor to know and act upon it. Parceled out as we near the edge of our own abyss, it can only do so much. If not embraced universally, it may prove to be too little, too late. Our traditions inform us about the power of illusion or Maya. They teach how it separates us from the essential reality within. I see Cao Pi glimpsing at truth for only the sliver of a thin moment. For him, a man of action, it was enough to turn the course of destiny for Cao Zhi — and for the counselors and their otherwise innocent families. We take two things from this lesson. First, trust that in compassion, righteousness will follow. Second, weigh fully the consequences of your actions, and the impact they have on all which you value. Compassion's sword can surprise. It may cut both ways. Nothing is certain. When you abandon compassion to suit your needs, it is perhaps you who will feel the ultimate sting of her unexpected tail's turn."

Zhi Mei asked, "But how does that help us today? How do we find contentment in your words? What are you saying about life?"

Bao Ling looked to her, "I am real, you are real, compassion exists. Maya spins the three into uncertainty. It is for us, and not Maya to choose when to move. It's not easy. And when we act, it is for us to do so decisively. I'm not entirely sure what it means in the end. But for now, it's all we have."

After due consideration, Zhi Mei could only nod in acknowledgment. She wasn't sure what it meant either, but could think of no further questions.

As they continued onward with their journey, Zhi Mei's song of lament to Cao Zhi resonated from beneath the tree cover reaching far to the hills beyond.

A young poet sighs
Alone, speaking to the winds
Words blown to four directions
Reminisce a princely brother's affections

Spirits lifted to clouds high
Heaven perhaps, gone awry
Quiet this humor, sullen within,
Where is my wrong, for this, what sin?

Walking north, blown south

Walking east, blown west
Lifted by whirlwinds glimpsing heaven's end
Striking ceilings of life's cruel rend

Show me the one heart way
Where peace and harmony rule the day
Roots seek roots running deep
While stalks burn and brothers forgotten weep

The Poet Zhi Mei

A Masterpiece

By late morning, the tree line drifted from view as they entered the high alpine. Patches of snow blanketed distant ridges to their front. The eastern sun had yet to light the ravines. With their ascent, the air chilled considerably. Fortunately, they remained comfortably warmed by the exertion. The trail gradually wound and thinned. Drop offs became more prevalent. At times, the path narrowed to where it barely accommodated the now cautious steps of the mules. Initially, Zhi Mei made light of their apprehension. She wondered if Bao Ling joked when he admonished, "We should respect them and their instincts. They are doing what they do to warn us to take more care. I've learned to mind their signals, and to respect their courtesy."

At times, Crystal Springs Temple swung momentarily into view. Glimpsed in bits and fragments as they rounded a bend, or crossed an intervening ridge. By then, they were high above the lowland river planes. With its eternal snow cap, Southern Mountain lit brightly in the far south.

In such places, eyes can play tricks. The temple seemed close. More than once Bao Ling predicted it would be just beyond the next rocky outcrop. Only to turn a corner and see it still floating majestically in the far distance.

Come mid-afternoon, they ascended into the high country. Making peace with the now thinned air, their breathing slowed to deliberate and measured. Though a lowlander, Bao Ling had become accustomed to this. Wandering the high and remote reaches of Southern Mountain with Sying Hao had forged his stamina. He often joked to his friend how he too had become a mountain goat.

At some point, the streaming songs of Zhi Mei quieted. Breath came before verse. They continued in silence to the rhythm of the animals amidst the dancing breezes.

By late day, they traversed a series of cutbacks sawing upwards over yet another steep hillside. Finally emerging at the top they found an immense gorge spread wide before them. They saw only a frail rope bridge. It appeared to be anchored into giant rock faces on both sides. Bao Ling turned to Zhi Mei, "I don't like the looks of this." He walked along the edge and heard the roaring turbulence from water racing far below. A river raged at the bottom. His attention was suddenly drawn to Zhi Mei, now vomiting in the rear. He knew the symptoms. His own head throbbed and spun from the combined effects of exertion and altitude.

"It will take several days for our bodies to adjust. The discomfort will gradually ease. Best we stop for now. Take rest. Pushing forward today will only make it worse."

Early next morning, they thoroughly scouted the area.

She looked toward him, concern evident, "Can we cross this?"

"I don't know. Perhaps there's another way." Bao Ling was having second thoughts about taking on this delivery mission to Abbott Shi-Hui Ke. But he also knew the problem wasn't the fulfillment. Having Zhi Mei and the animals along had complicated everything. Alone, he would already have crossed.

She answered, "In these mountains, there's usually more than one way for everything. But where?" She stared over the edge then scanned far left and right. Realizing the predicament, she questioned, "Will we have the time to find it?"

"No, unfortunately we won't. We don't know what's out there, and we can't second guess what we already see. Do you think you can stay here alone with the animals? If I continue ahead, perhaps I can find someone to guide us."

Bao Ling didn't express it, but she knew from his words. He didn't trust the bridge to bear their combined weight, or the added weight of the animals.

It sat in the shrouded distance, nestled in the formidable rocks and harbored from wind and ill weather by surrounding ridges. Bao Ling saw the true majesty of the temple for the first time. It stood as a complex edifice, perfectly integrated into the hostile surround. Some parts stood readily visible, others tucked into the shadows. He also detected evidence of planting and cultivation in painstakingly adjoined plateaus of fertility. These patches of field were carefully positioned to trap light. Set precisely to gather every glimmer of sunshine from above. Bao Ling counted nine more footbridges barely visible in the turns and shadows once across the gorge. He noted carefully how they were arranged to confuse the eye and misdirect anyone who thought to sneak entry into the compound. They looked to lead nowhere. A carefully calculated arrangement of purpose and deception. Each hilltop, crest and ridge floated independently atop a vast sea of clouds. He would have to reconcile this indeterminate maze. A conundrum meant to divide and weaken any larger force harboring ill will.

There may have been others yet unseen, for there seemed to be no end. This represented far more than a temple. It was indeed a carefully conceived community, and no mean accomplishment considering the challenges. Fingers of steaming water could be seen descending the rocky face beneath the main building. Trailing down the hillsides until vanishing into the emptiness of the ravine below. They seemed almost dreamlike. Evaporating before ever touching bottom. Bao Ling immediately recognized the signs of warmed waters from the mountain's heart. He knew then the compound to be a nearly impregnable fortress. Able to survive even the coldest of harsh mountain winters. Here it rested unassailable as the western-most gateway for the interior Shu trails and passes. Sying Hao, alone on the opposing bank, could hold off an entire army single handedly. Never needing more than his skills as an archer.

He knew the compound could never have been built, nor could it have survived, depending only on traffic and supplies crossing the meager rope bridge. For certain, other entries and crossings existed. He carefully scanned the adjoining hillsides and the walls of the ravine. He had no answers. *This riddle is the work of a consummate artist and a magician.* His mind settled quickly onto the one single possibility. *Zhuge Liang!* He remembered Sying Hao's admonition that one could spend an eternity trying to unravel Zhuge Liang's puzzles. They were better met with admiration. Appreciated, and not challenged! For Bao Ling, it felt on this day he had met the wizard firsthand!

Laughing at the uncanny wonder of it all, he returned to Zhi Mei.

She questioned, "What's so funny?"

Bal Ling answered, "We have before us a great masterpiece. I am laughing at my own insignificance in relation to the scope of its brilliance, and possibilities."

Quick to the bit, she asked, "There's more to this than meets the eye, isn't there?"

"Yes, so much more as to defy one's imagination.

"We will camp here for the night, allow ourselves to fully adjust to the changes. I will cross the bridge in the morning and announce myself to Abbot Shi-Hui Ke. I expect he will tell us what to do next."

"What if he doesn't?"

"Then I will do what I came to do, and we will depart."

She looked to Bao Ling, "What is this mission Sying Hao has bound you to?"

Bao Ling paused. Wheels turned within, kneading the question of what Zhi Mei should be told.

Impatiently, she asked again.

He looked to her. Knowing that apart from his dreams of returning one day to Ling Village, she was his only thread to the thought of continuing on. Slowly he walked to his things and returned with the pouch.

He put it in her hands. "I am to deliver this to Abbot Shi-Hui Ke. I am told to trust he will make it right."

Zhi Mei felt the great weight within. Barely able to lift it, she returned it unopened to Bao Ling, in whose hands it moved as though weightless.

"You didn't choose to look?" he asked.

"Not necessary. What is there is what is there. The hopes and dreams of simple people. Torn from their hands by fiends. But how did it get to you?"

"Are you sure you want to know?"

She answered with a firm nod.

"You might recall. Several days ago, in town, there was talk of a missing purse. Presumably funding for forces advancing into the west and re-connecting with the silk road. It had been mysteriously lifted from a company of soldiers en route to their provincial overlord. They entered our refuge ..."

"Your refuge?"

"Southern Mountain, which I share with all creatures in peace, and with ghosts," he smiled mischievously to her.[4]

"Some things shouldn't be mocked," she pouted, feigning anger.

"Living on the mountain as we do, Sying Hao and I are acutely aware of any changes. This is especially so with Sying Hao. It's as though he reads the winds and the waters. From the subtle changes he can sense what and who approaches. Even when they are one or two days out. That's how we came upon the trespassing soldiers. We found their camp. When night fell, Sying Hao made his way into their midst. I watched and waited should he require my assistance. I witnessed as he dallied among them. To my

---

[4] In our two previous works, *Seed of Dragons*, and *Token Tales and Fragments* we first meet Sying Hao. He appears unexpectedly. A mysterious elder who befriends the outlaw Bao Ling. Somehow knowing of Bao Ling's past, he offers refuge, inviting the young man to share his hideaway on Southern Mountain. Like an older brother Sying Hao takes his new friend under wing, carefully adding the finishing touches on all Bao Ling needs to know for whatever lies ahead. Not surprisingly, locals speak of ghosts roaming the mountain. One in particular, named Sying Hao.

eyes, he seemed to be one of them. Even to the extent of sitting in their midst and eating with them. He went about unimpeded and unchallenged as far as I could see.

My feeling he knew them turned out to be an illusion. Later, to my disbelief, he told me he had gone undetected. I didn't know what he meant or what to think. I saw what I saw. Part of me wanted to think he was gaming me. My doubts lingered, though I didn't dispute or show skepticism when he carefully explained what he did. I now know his account to have been the truth, hard as it was at first to accept. He returned afterward with this pouch. When I realized what he had, I knew it was no accidental undertaking. Sying Hao read their heart's intent long before they arrived. He knew how to turn the evil back onto itself. This pouch, their harvest of oppression — he simply lifted from their midst, then set a new course for its eventual return."

"And Abbot Shi-Hu Ke is the vehicle for this endeavor?"

"Uncle Wei assures me of his integrity."

"Then it is so."

Crystal Springs Trail

Come first light, Bao Ling readied to cross the bridge.

Zhi Mei seemed less settled than usual. Did she have reservations about having to stay behind? She said nothing of it. While they ate, Bao Ling sensed her reticence but was at a loss for words.

Then again, it might have been lack of sleep. Wild animals could be heard roving about throughout the night. Thinking this the cause, he tried to calm her. He told of scavengers and their nocturnal habits. "They constantly search for food and prey. Our mules and edibles are new to them. A powerful draw. It's not unusual. Most night creatures pose no threat beyond their curiosity."

She countered, "In this wilderness, not all creatures are insignificant. Besides, I heard you treading about in the darkness. What were you up to?"

He might have misspoken. He asked whether she heard the bears rummaging through the camp. That is, until he woke to chase them off.

"Bears? How many were there?"

"Let's find out."

He escorted her through the camp site. Together, they looked about for signs. He showed how he read tracks and markings. "See there! The bit of hair on the bush." He picked at it, then spun it between his fingertips. Coarse and rough to the touch, he concluded "Definitely an older bear." They meticulously studied all they found. Methodically, they scoured for more signs in the brush. She marveled at how he ultimately proved in convincing fashion — "There had been three. No more than that."

"Just three?" she asked. "Well, that's not so bad!"

Bao Ling didn't know what to make of her words. Perhaps a light serving of sarcasm. Playing safe, and for added good measure, he stressed, "You'll be fine. I'll be back before dark. You won't be alone tonight. But don't forget. Even in daylight, stay close to the mules. Their protective instincts will include you and the communal territory. But you must remain near. Trust them. They are quite capable."

Zhi Mei's stare in response made it clear she was nobody's rube. He was saying what she already knew. He smiled in surrender, hoping to disarm her.

The time came to set off. His instincts sounded constant alarms as neared the bridge. His suspicions were triggered. Who could tell what surprises might lurk. Should he even trust it? *What would Sying Hao do?*

With that thought, a change of heart. He called Zhi Mei to the crossing point. "A slight shift in plans." Removing the pouch from across his shoulder, he held it out to her. "You'd better safeguard this."

"Why not take it with you?"

"It's extra weight. You can see how the bridge worries me. Why be careless and risk losing it now? Should anything happen, I know you'll do what's right."

She stalled momentarily trying to wrap her thoughts around his words. From this close vantage point, she gradually came to understand. The bridge simply accepted those who could decipher its secrets. Or who and whatever those on the other side determined fit to cross. They had seeded it with traps and pitfalls throughout. Counting bears told of high skill, but this new challenge?

She now grasped what he wanted and why. He was asking, as much as telling. They did not have the luxury of trusting chance or disregarding ill fortune. A cold gust of air made her shudder. *These might be our last words together.*

He smiled warmly as she nodded her understanding and assent. She smiled back. They were partners after all. More words would have added nothing.

Treading lightly, he made his way timidly at first. Warily, he set and timed each delicate step onto the aged planks. Some shifted. Some cracked. Some tilted or gave way beneath his weight. Occasionally, one or two held firm and he edged forward. He would know which to trust only after he stepped. No read came easy. The craft and cleverness of the edifice were evident. Anyone could see it required constant monitoring and mending. He suspected there existed a sure path across. One which if properly mapped or memorized would purchase firm footing. He did not have that prior advantage. He held no privy to its secrets. Several times his feet pushed through the planks. With each close call, he stopped to catch his breath. And to stare through what might have been.

Imagination likes to play tricks. He had visions of suddenly dropping down. Then sensing the sluggishness of disaster time as he accelerated in hopeless free fall. The raging stream far below grew until it filled the vision. Its certain promise — a quick finish at the bottom. He wondered as to his final thoughts should he fall. Then he knew! He'd be worrying about Zhi Mei. He smiled at the thought. In the moment, only his iron grip on the cables secured him from that fate.

After experiencing the failure of what he at first deemed a solid and "true" plank, he inspected the remnants. Within them, he found evidence of intentional cuts set beneath. *A trap for the unwary, or the too impatient!* He also saw how the supports and anchors on the eastern bank were configured. Set for quick release. A single sword stroke could undo the entire edifice. Those stranded aboard would be entrapped. Dispatched to their inevitable doom. He made it a point to remember his steps and the sure footings. He would need them for his return. Should he be so fortunate.

Over at last, he found the trail ahead empty and clear. An easy tread, but for the steep ascent. Continuing, he detected signs of utility and function incorporated into the surrounds. The clear hand of habitation could be seen everywhere. He reckoned how these changes likely evolved over a period spanning generations, perhaps longer. Whoever laid claim to these remote spaces seemed accustomed to having them exclusively to themselves.

Movements of water trickled from higher ice fields. They coalesced into streams and rivulets everywhere he scanned. Their murmurs permeated the atmosphere, a degree of added serenity. *It seems the mountain has a chant of its own.* In other spots, pools emitted steam, affirming the presence of thermal springs. Looking more closely, he saw additional evidence of rigorous organization and planning. Each patch of arable soil had been systematically nurtured, terraced, shaped and stepped. Guided by human hands to productive use over time. Fed by flows of water from carefully engineered lines and trenches running from both within and above. As he progressed, he noticed broad arrays of medicinal herbs cultivated and painstakingly groomed. Among the many, wolfberry, known for enhancing Yin, governing resistance to illness. Elsewhere, yellow leader, used to address deficiencies of respiration. Ginseng, of course, and hawthorn for stagnation and circulation.

Bao Ling possessed far more than the typical hunter's basic field knowledge of healing plants. He could properly brew, process, prescribe and administer. In his village he had spent much time with elders. Medicine men and women who oversaw the community's health and wellbeing. He hunted frequently and spent considerable time afield. They counted on him to collect plants for their needs and purposes. A high responsibility, they allowed no margin for error in judgment. He developed a true eye and learned the lessons well.

Not infrequently, illness to others required he journey remotely into the distant wilderness. There he might seek out some obscure fungus, or perhaps mushrooms changed by parasites into new entities. Some glowed red. They appeared like lobsters crawling on the forest floor. He watched and learned as village masters brewed and mixed carefully. Occasionally they added pinches of earth or nail cuttings (which they jokingly referred to as unicorn horn) — even, to his disbelief, animal dung, or other unmentionables. As a young man, he often wondered how the elders had come to their vast knowledge. *How many remedies must have been tried and discarded? What transpired before one concluded some rare find at the bottom of a pond, or some repulsive compound of waste and decay might heal the afflicted?* For the young archer, a process of great gravity and mystery. Benefits proven with time, and countless trials and repetitions.

Though sometimes repulsed by what he saw going into the compounds, he witnessed firsthand how the concoctions benefited the ill and stricken. Encouraged by the elders, he trained his memory to lock the knowledge within himself for future use. In simple communal societies, skills like these are passed readily to those willing to learn. Most importantly, those able to engage what they have have been taught. Not all can achieve that.

Some of the elders recognized his potential early on. They were careful to instruct him on the relationships of the five elements. Then the four winds and the flow of chi under the influence of yin and yang within. An unwitting apprentice, in his mind, he deserved nothing for doing only what he felt to be his job. Perhaps for that reason, he viewed these lessons to be gifts precious as jewels. Once gotten, they were carefully guarded so as to never be forgotten. In that way, they would be preserved and again in time, propagated to others.

It was because of these teachings Bao Ling first committed himself to mastering the ancient script. A side benefit: he eventually learned to read and write. He routinely made light of his efforts to perfect these skills. What he gained propelled him far beyond what his contemporaries were capable of accomplishing. Gradually he grew more confident. He began scribing the formulas and ingredients for the concoctions. Preserving the many bits and pieces, he amassed a collection reminiscent of works preserved from the time of the Yellow Emperor. Timid, and wanting not to offend, he let years slip before ultimately sharing with the elders. To his surprise, they were overjoyed at his initiative. They encouraged he continue, assuring he was performing a great service for the common good. *Such a fine young man,* they thought.

Of course, competing warlords and their goons[5] relegated much of that record to the same fires which

---

[5] Ling Village, where Bao Ling was raised and nurtured had been completely overrun and pillaged by warlords and competing armies.

consumed the bones of the elders. Devastated by this, in the aftermath Bao Ling kept what he knew to himself. It pained him to even think of it. Or the memories.

It was Sying Hao who re-opened this once sealed link to his past. Apparently, Sying Hao saw him foraging about. No doubt, he read its meaning. He was taken and surprised by what Bao Ling already knew regarding the properties of medicinal plants and fungi. Before long, he urged Bao Ling to again produce from memory what he had recorded previously. Then to Bao Ling's re-emerging delight, Sying Hao shared his own similar efforts. He had amassed volumes of carefully preserved findings and records of explorations. Knowledge gleaned from a lifetime of close observations and experiments. Exploring the collections, Bao Ling marveled at their scope and the many samples and specimens. What he found had come from Sying Hao's direct personal experiences. *If I had spent every waking moment doing the same, I could not have produced even a fraction of his record. How was it possible?* he wondered.

You can surely understand the dilemma he faced in the moment. He had committed for his mission to Shi-Hui Ke. He had already promised a return to Zhi Mei that evening. On any other day, he would have yielded to the temptation to pause. He had never seen the likes of it. If only he could better understand the planning behind these hillside and valley plots. How could they exist in this environment? No doubt, they would yield a golden harvest promising great benefit to anyone who knew just how. But, in his other mind, he saw no inhabitants. He wondered over their absence. For him, a sure sign not to delay or be careless.

As he finally neared, the temple compound grew larger and more intricate. He scanned the broad surrounds. They were carpeted with assortments of edibles. Many looked to be wild, others carefully cultivated. Though situated in the high country, he saw ravines, dips and descending slopes — all mounted within a sweeping plateau. Little worlds in themselves, each a suitable locale for chosen plants to thrive. Endless possibilities, given the many orchestrated permutations of environment and climate. His own people of course knew these practices well. For that reason, he recognized them. Over time, villagers learned from endless repetition. No matter how limited the venue, or difficult the terrain. There could always be found subtle variations in sunlight, rain and wind exposure. Even within parcels closely adjacent or separated by a few chi[6] of altitude. Over the course of generations, with collective memory, people learned what to plant, and where.

He could see how these monks and the surrounding community had done more with little than he had ever deemed possible: the cultivated plants, supplemented by the wild bounty, the nuts, the pines, the fungi. There were probably even fish in what seemed carefully dammed pools. His imagination ran with the possibilities. One could survive in this fortress indefinitely.

---

[6] In modern times, cultures which use the measure define it to be one-third of a meter, or approximately 1 ft 1 in. It can be further subdivided into Chinese inches, or cun, with 10 cun equaling 1 chi. During the period of our stories, a chi would have worked out to about 9.5 inches.

The last several li of his trip passed quickly. He kept his purpose focused. The wonders of this heavenly citadel could easily have overwhelmed his curiosity and blanketed his commitments. He would not be further distracted.

Part 2

So Many Lessons

Monkey Discovers Buddha

The main temple perched amidst clusters of geologic monoliths. The spaces surrounding worked with and against the monoliths resulting in an ebb and flow of shadows and light which confused perception. Zhuge Liang had a well deserved reputation for evoking illusions such as this. During his heyday, entire armies were known to have wandered helplessly about. Disoriented for days. All sense of direction stolen while prey made good their escape.

The terrain challenges would have been discouragement enough. On approach, Bao Ling descended a long gradient cleared between two rocky prominences. These walls channeled whoever came thru into full-frontal view. The field narrowed tightly to his front. A force intent on laying siege would be bottlenecked before establishing their launch. Natural ambush points surrounded the descent. Drawing closer, he crossed a final expanse of semi cultivated field. Vulnerable and exposed, he was again reminded of traps and the reason for impediments. Bao Ling already knew his presence and slowed progress had been detected. A wary glance to the rear ... *Am I being followed?*

He recognized the temple to be a daoguan[7]. A learned eye would know by the exterior it had begun to absorb and integrate the influences of Buddhism. From Sying Hao, Bao Ling learned how Buddhism first entered the land. It came remotely from a distant land. Far beyond the great mountains of the remote south. One might suppose — from another world. Early in its emergence, it had been well received among the western nomads. Spreading with goods in trade, seeds of the new teachings hitched aboard eastbound caravans. Carried from who knows where into the heart of the empire. Many spilled along the way. Orphan seedlings sprouted their own separate paths spidering into the heartlands. From there they flourished and spread even beyond. Webs touching everywhere, penetrating every heart. Was it a faith, or simply a new perspective on reality? That question might still be debated. Regardless, the new tide nudged its forward wave uninhibited. So convincing were the doctrines, they gained the full support of late Han's esteemed notables, particularly Emperor Ming.

Wishing to learn all he could of these new teachings, the emperor ordered his ambassadors to make the great journey to the west. "Find the source!" he commanded. They were to secure all deemed missing from first glimpses into this new formula for truth. He viewed the potentials a matter of national interest. They could not be ignored. For the many sent, an impossible task. Some concluded, "Beyond human capacity." A great number did not survive. Their efforts and determination cannot be overstated. Nor can their sacrifices. They crossed the great land and experienced

---

[7] A Taoist temple.

monumental hardships. The strongest few managed to traverse the terrible and unforgiving southern ranges. The same mountains which once nearly finished off the venerable Liu Bei.

They are rightfully credited with delivering the great truth to the homeland. There, with the Emperor's encouragement and mandate, the teachings spread quickly. For the population, they constituted a new view on life and circumstance. A reconciliation of suffering into purpose. Hope for the many. Certainly, the Emperor, as a practical leader, saw all this as means to an end. Contentment among his people promised peace and security. With peace and security, prosperity would follow. As though an answer conceived in preparation for troubles already brewing. From beneath the surface, Buddhism took full root and blossomed into radiance.

The sages in the remote subcontinent should be acknowledged. To their credit, they withheld nothing from those who survived the journey west. You see, the emissaries bore great rewards. Their mission met fine reception. Honored by all for the difficulty of its undertaking. They eventually returned home with troves of gifted scrolls. Endless road maps for new awakenings, along with timeless collections of sutras. Insights intended to fully nourish kindred spirits in the lands far to the north. No doubt, rulers in the south were also practical leaders. They reckoned the obvious. With correct thinking and a firm grip on reality, no one among the Northerners would be so carelessly inclined as to infringe on a neighbor. Particularly one so remote.

These treasures as well as the expedition itself were said to have been under the direct charge and protection of a Colonel Sun. We believe this to be the very same man as Sying Hao's one time mentor and father companion. But who can be sure? Admittedly, Bao Ling had never been able to square the expedition's history and timing with what he calculated should have been Sun's likely physical age. Somehow the numbers went askew. He would have to find a way to reconcile the computations. Otherwise, nothing would ever make sense. Sying Hao of course, had his own take on the matter.

He told how the journey to the west had been an epic endeavor. It spanned years, and only a small portion of those who ambitiously set out ever returned. The honored treasures crossed through the homeland on the backs of noble white steeds. Always under the vigilant eye of Sun. In the remote west, anything could happen. Storms, marauders, thirst, disease, theft or abandonment, to name a few. Some of the artifacts had even been lost to quicksand. Not a day passed without Sun fearing for their safety and preservation. From the caravan's first descent into the remote desert wastelands, Sun took steps to ensure the records would survive. Even in the event he should not make it. He elicited the aid of Taoist monks and hermits. Dropouts from civilization populating the desert emptiness. These eminent scholars carefully copied and replicated the scrolls at multiple waypoints along the grinding return.

Among those assisting, some found themselves completely overcome by what they read while copying. Not a few attained full realization on the spot! The proof can sometimes be in the mix as they say. Before it could be contained or controlled, their own influence fanned outward like a wildfire! New awarenesses and awakenings rippled north and south alongside the return trail. Temples and shrines sprouted in their wake. It brought joy to Sun, and immense wonder to the many others. What had been unleashed? What sort of power were they witnessing?

Understandably, the great journey ended in wide anticipation and acclaim. Colonel Sun rightfully became the subject of tales and folk legends[8]. So much so, in time people of the land disassociated the actual Colonel Sun from the achievement. They spun their own magic, attributing it to their "Monkey King." We've no doubt our Sun would have shuddered at the thought.

Taoists, finding great merit and wisdom in these new scriptures harbored the suspicion old Laozi had ended up in the subcontinent. There, he somehow connected with the Gautama Buddha. Perhaps the two were one and same? By the time the entourage had crossed the final west-east mountain ranges, enough essential copies had been made to ensure their spread throughout the land. Events unfolded as though having their own will. The pearls would survive, no matter what. Whatever course the minds of men and emperors might later take, these teachings would continue.

Yes, it does happen. When it suits their ends and inclinations, some leaders will purge entire realms of truth and clarity. Keeping the masses helpless and confused suits their advantage. Sying Hao would often say, "Colonel Sun

---

[8] Memorialized many centuries later by Wu Cheng'en in his "Journey to the West."

was no Shithead. He had real brains and always moved with a compassionate purpose and to full effect. If not for him, the teachings would already have been excised from our awarenesses. Once gone, we'd be staring only at dark deception."

Sying Hao told how the trying journey had unexpectedly changed Sun. Before the pilgrimage, he was long proven to be a fearless and uncompromising warrior. He gleefully welcomed any challenge. Rarely did the consequences concern him. A death wish perhaps? Within the court, rumors spread of him being an ancient spirit. Perhaps for that reason, he stood detached from greed of the moment or the commonality of self-perpetuating ambition. He harbored a fierce demeanor sprinkled with unpredictability, fronted by a not always welcoming simian scowl. The combination chilled the spleens of anyone wishing to better know, or to befriend him. By his own choice he existed within himself. Did he like it? Who can say? A revenant left over from some long gone and forgotten age. Could it be he descended from beings who no longer trod the earth? But for the likes of him, his kind would never have been known to exist. "A seeming castaway on the sea of eternity." That's what the Emperor's counselors whispered. They would have been shocked to learn how close they had come to the truth. They didn't like him. In fact, they feared both what they knew and what they could never fathom of him. For the great Ming however, Colonel Sun represented the perfect choice to head the task. As an added benefit, the warrior would be away from the capital. There'd be less mischief and jealousy to contend with.

According to Sying Hao, the journey to the west brought Sun to his final refinement. That was the change he mentioned. A by-product or consequence of an epic undertaking. The unending trials of the journey, along with new experiences in the subcontinent, forged Sun's actualized end state. In the new land, he discovered other peoples. Many as different in their appearance as he himself had been from those in the north. He often recalled seeing people with blue skin, or skin of many hues. Then told of great princes with untold wealth, as well as starving children ignored on nameless streets at nightfall. He recalled lepers at palace gates, and mendicants walking about in the wilderness seeking enlightenment. And the sacred streams, which defied imagination. Some born high in remote mountain retreats. A place where holy men bathed and meditated. He even joined them at times, recalling how they saw his battle-scarred body, and had the courtesy not to ask or comment. A rare demonstration of restraint which he appreciated.

He learned of ancient peoples, apart even from the Buddhists. Some appeared to be of his kind, whose combined legacies were meticulously scribed and preserved in urns buried throughout the land. These artifacts were constantly being surfaced or discovered. Mostly by serendipity as old soils were turned or washed away. He spoke of great insights and lessons preserved in these treasures. They had been recorded in a script he could not at first decipher, but apparently of ancient origin and common to the subcontinent. He found others who could with study and effort lay bare the mysteries. Sun marveled how the script, unlike the pictographs and logo grams of his own culture, went straight to the sound, and left much less to conjecture as to the meaning.

He shared how he had met with what he deemed ordinary men and women, same flesh and blood as us. Noble spirits who had somehow poked and peeked through the barriers between the many worlds. In accomplishing this, they learned all which cut to and through the core of human and religious experience. "Simplicity itself!" he would say. "So simple in fact, it cannot be easily taught or replicated. In our world, they'd likely be proclaimed saints, perhaps gods. Titles they would simply laugh over and ignore. Just as they continued moving along and tooting their flutes." He learned the great simplicity to be, "What we think of as death is not the termination or conclusion of existence. In like fashion, what we think to be life is not the substance or act of existence. Somewhere in between is the direct unified experience of the eternal. Everything stands mid-stream in the solitary moment." So simple a truth, so impossible to grasp! That's where this Buddhism became so very important to all. It was never to be an easy path for the unwary, or the unwilling.

Treasures Atop Noble Steeds

When he first heard Sying Hao reference the "somewhere in between," Bao Ling recalled once before crossing paths with the expression. It summoned his childhood, and fond memories of Iron Hand Gao[9]. What might be the connection?

Per Sying Hao, from the first Colonel Sun made it his practice to receive the teachings by immersion. That meant, tapping the source. He insisted always on sitting in with his teams of scholars and academics. He had no interest in their reports, summaries, or conclusions. He figured by screening the scrolls directly, he would internalize the teachings firsthand. No intermediaries. No interpretations or false trails. He marveled at the beauty and complexity of awareness and understanding radiating from the script. He wondered, *Could anyone's insights be so profound?* And yet,

---

[9] Bao Ling once found his teacher, Iron Hand Gao, seemingly dead, cold and rigid after an evening of heavy weather. The apparent passing became a teaching point for the old master. He told the child he had been "somewhere in between." The full account can be found in *Seed of Dragons*.

he seemed to understand — to lock grip with the essential
message. Sun remembered how the collected scholars
would read segments, then stop to savor the lesson. Before
long, they started their thinking. And with that would
commence incessant debating over what was in fact meant
or intended. It couldn't be avoided. People are like that.
Particularly scholars. Within each of us can be found a
completely unique conceptual environment. Not
infrequently, a seed planted in one will produce fruit quite
different from that same seed planted in another.

It took only a few days when some of these first friendly
exchanges became heated. By week's end, different camps
of collective thought became apparent within the group. In
fact, but for the stern and admonishing yellow-fire eyes of
Colonel Sun, the emissaries may very well have run their
mission hard aground with their internecine infighting.
They struggled hard amongst themselves trying to peg who
had the true understanding. Who among them stood best
qualified to interpret the great doctrine once they returned
to the imperial court? You see, with interpretations come
recognition. With recognition, one accrues power and
status! Clearly, great teachings can have their traps.

The group failed to discern one important development.
In their very midst, a change had unfolded in the normally
taciturn and sullen Colonel Sun. While others lounged,
courted, indulged and cajoled their hosts, Sun roamed the
countryside and hills. He sought to assimilate every
experience and lesson into what he now referred to as "his
consciousness of the moment." Fascinated with the
mechanics of the ancient language, he worked tirelessly to
master its intricacies. As months flew, he came to

remarkable skill in deciphering the timeless messages. You must understand. Though base in his appearance and sometimes brutish in approach, Colonel Sun was as broad in his intellect as he was in his physical skills. Nothing of merit escaped his discerning eye. And inasmuch as he was already freed of ambition and distraction, we conjecture his spirit, above all the others, lay fertile for proper seed to take root. Might that also explain why he had been expressly designated by the emperor to lead the expedition?

It started when he and the emissaries first delved into the scrolls. The disciplined Sun shut out all distractions and continued reading intently. *This becomes something I do for myself.* He could hear them debating at first, then arguing. Their voices little more than token annoyances in the background. Manifesting like the squawk of chickens, arguing incessant nonsense. He had no further interest in their interpretations. What came from their beaks no longer meant anything to him. Just sounds floating about — no beginnings, no endings, no real substance, no true import. Just chickens mumbling. Instead, the powerful words before his focused gaze propelled images as arrows exploding lightning-like over fields of dreams and dew within. Time ceased. He became one with the texts. Even with the distracting mumbles in the background. He could have stayed suspended in that state forever. And in fact had thought to do just that. *Had I not already witnessed an enlightened child sitting in the recess of a bo tree for weeks at a time. Never leaving to eat or drink or to eliminate? Yes ... suspended forever, why not?*

But a promise is a promise. At least to one so noble as Sun. After delighting in emptiness for a seeming eternity, he knew to let it go. *Why have it become yet another object of desire?* As he re-emerged into the moment, surrounding sounds of chickens squawking re-formed into words. Once again, they plagued his senses. Surprisingly, nothing remained within them to any longer give offense. Had there been a shift? Had he become different?

He turned to the group. "You're missing the point!" he bellowed. Then for added emphasis, punctuated with his bone chilling earth vibrating growl.

Terrified, all drew silent. No one would deny the attention seemingly demanded. To everyone's surprise and relief, Sun only smiled to the group. Then he stood, bowed politely and left.

They had never seen him smile before. The unexpectedly warm glow soothed their spirits. Some remained that way for several days following. One of life's miracles.

Colonel Sun had reconnected with compassion. Perhaps under the guiding but unseen inspiration of Guanyin. In the endless battles and fruitless military campaigns, Sun came to awarenesses few others achieved. First among them, how conflict rings its own bells, takes its own tolls, and unfolds to its own ends. Rarely is any achievement permanently gained or won. Yet losses accrue to all. He knew this from trial and direct experience. Without the underlying causes first being addressed and remedied, and the once opponents steering themselves to tolerance and respect, no peace can ever hold.

But it went beyond that. The doors of perception dropped completely from their hinges when Sun came to terms with the underlying reality of Guanyin. You see, for others, Colonel Sun included, she was yet another of the celestials. Just like all of the other gods, part of an administrative hierarchy not unlike that of the imperial court. There were gods in charge of lightning, agriculture, food, valor, conflict, salvation. Even horses. Well, given the state of affairs as they were, Guanyin managed compassion. A very low office indeed — at least for the gods. For them status meant everything. Sun liked to think of her as a woman, but prior history shows men had already tried to hijack the role. At least in the portrayals. So, some pictured Guanyin as a woman; some pictured her as a man; some compromised and pictured her as both. Sun liked that.

He found people often choose to externalize and bastardize characteristics which are otherwise integral to and inherent to their very natures. They do this instead of what they should be doing — the work. Nurturing and actualizing the trait within. Why? Simply because it's so much easier to put it out there where it can be worshiped. As you'll find in what follows, it leads to no end of devilry. Sun had transformed. He now knew Guanyin's embodiment of compassion did not stand apart from him. It was him! It came from him and had to be ignited from within by his choice, his will, and his actions. Let others play games with it as they wished. Paint deities over it. Have it appear in the form of a benevolent fairy. Call it man, woman or something in between. No sooner are they done, when it floats away. Colonel Sun had brought it home. Now he found it was always there. Like a lifeline always within easy reach for each of us, as we drifted about like flotsam on

chaotic and uncertain seas. Consider this. One as hardened
as Sun could choose to change. Cannot we too? If only we,
like he, knew what to look for, and to act decisively once it
neared our grasp.

Colonel Sun remained forever among the warriors
supreme. But his sword acquired a compassionate edge
from that day. As commander of the mission, he assumed
full responsibility for the scriptures. He would not have
them lost through carelessness, arrogance, or stupidity. On
first return to the homeland, he transported the treasures
atop noble steeds. No one who saw could mistake their
profound significance. He ordered the scholars to prepare
meticulous inventories. In the end, with the Emperor's
blessing, they were housed permanently at what came to be
the White Horse Temple. The shrine stands to this day.

Standing Like a Post

Who knows why things happen as they do? In the moments Bao Ling closed on the temple's portico, thoughts of Sun enticed his curiosity. It seemed a ghostly presence beckoned him forward. But to what purpose or end? Scriptures? He forced his attention to the intricate frontage. Gilded gold set over red trim. Rippling green dragons reached to the far edges and corners. *Focus on the job at hand,* he thought. Glazed tiles glowing golden adorned the roof. Or perhaps just the sunlight tricking his eyes. An assortment of frontal panels were covered in frescoes. Bao Ling recognized the images as visual metaphors for each of the 64 trigrams of the Yi Ching.

Sying Hao had once shared how interpretations from the yarrow stalks might be more perceptively delineated using visual imagery. "It's far preferable to parsing words and apparent surface contradictions. One must struggle to push toward truth through verse." He shared samples of such images with Bao Ling, explaining they were produced by masters. "Their understanding went deep into the essential realities. To the very rivers upon which everything else rested and flowed." The images here brought those memories back. Bao Ling wondered if they came from the same hands.

Passing through the portico, he entered a sweeping courtyard. He had stepped into a new world. Spread upon the field of tile before him were characterizations of the astrological families. He could make out the spirit symbols for each of the constellations, all carefully recorded. Their interplay skillfully mapped within the rainbow colors of stone and mortar on the vast surface to his front.

He reckoned one could learn a great deal simply by walking this courtyard over time. Then he discovered shadows thrown by the sunlight's passage through the columns. Nothing seemed unintended. He caught how the shadows angled and aligned with markers on the ground. He quickly deduced these were signposts for the seasons and indicators for the time of day. Looking closer, he saw how inscriptions in the courtyard instructed when to plant, when to gather, when to prepare and when to rest. All marked by the angled dance of celestial light and the pointing fingers of earthly shadows. Yang and Yin, the wheel of life. Mapped no doubt by an immortal's skilled and knowing hand.

The courtyard stood spacious and quiet as his studious eye roamed about. Though kept clean and functional, he could see it was regularly used by the residents. Bao Ling detected signs of martial play throughout. He found overlooked bits of arrow head. Also noted were ground scrapes and scuffs, presumably from staffs. Elsewhere, tiles had been worn thin by movements repeated endlessly. *Perhaps the practice of forms.* Even the posts, columns and passages had the inclination by design to serve as obstacle courses. Impediments when necessary, depending on who was present. Targeting strangers and unexpected visitors. Manipulating their approach to suit the community's chosen state of isolation.

He passed through yet another portico and found its rows of columns alongside directing him at long last to a formal entry. There a carefully suspended sign instructed, "Please be patient."

Odd, he thought. Framed by ascendant beams, the walls standing alongside and behind were embossed and colored with murals of prominent events. Maps of human affairs and the Empire's troubled history since the fall of Han. Bao Ling could make out portrayals of the Yellow Turban revolt. Nor did he miss Cao Cao's noble visage confidently overseeing the battlefield. In another, karmic retribution evident, Cao's imperial navy in flames beneath the death wind at Red Cliffs. The Yin and the Yang. And set between them stood Emperor Xian's edict. Written in his own blood. The very directive which precipitated the conspiracy against Cao Cao and ultimately spun the Empire into chaos. *Why would such portrayals be here? What nature of temple is this? A shrine to what?*

He stopped and stood immobile before the entrance, feet rooted firmly. *Expect anything.* Then he waited patiently — acting as the sign instructed. *They are watching.* After some time, perhaps hours, hearing or seeing nothing, he thought to pound on the door and demand attention. But for the mantra, commanded as polite persuasion, "Please be patient."

He saw nothing, heard nothing. *Am I being tested?*

In the past, Bao Ling had bristled at the suggestion he lacked patience. On this day, he almost felt the sign had been directed specifically at him and to no other. A suspicion he dismissed as impossible. Like all of us, he considered himself already a patient person. Just not one to be trifled with.

Truth be told, his patience barely exceeded that of a hungry dog. You see, after the desecration of Ling Village and the unrelenting pursuit mounted against him, little room remained for patience. All of his energy and focus went to the demands of survival. Like many driven to lives of reaction, he mistook his exceptional gift for survival as the calculated imbuement of patience with ruthless timing. For him, this accounted for the remarkable talent, or was it simple luck, which defined his edge over whatever came his way. You'll find in life patience is the heart of timing, and timing is where the wheel hits the road. The outlaw Bao Ling, alter ego Dragon of the Midlands, had great instincts for survival. Despite what he thought, in the beginning his timing had no heart, and no patience. Like most others on the run, eventually he would have met his sorry end. Sying Hao saw this and knew to gift him the art of patience. Actually, he taught him to master "standing like a post."

Long before encountering Sying Hao, Bao Ling had worked the many postures from the internal sciences. They had been transmitted to him by village elders. That included post standing. Typically, these concepts were passed down and preserved from one generation to the next.

They were always being scrutinized and tested, evolving and improving under influence from masters within the many communities. They could be simple, or complex. That depended on the intended use, or purpose. Some took inspiration from the spirit and qualities of animals. Standards among them were the tiger, the deer, the bear, the monkey and the crane. Others created physical geometries which might send healing or flushing energies. Contained within them, vibrations benefiting the five major organs: the liver, lung, spleen, heart, and kidney. When practiced diligently in association with proper breathing, benefits to health and dexterity were pronounced. Certainly, it was no accident they were in the end deadly effective and favored by martial artists.

The practices seemed always to have existed. Known since the earliest days. Legends tell how they were empirically formalized by Fu Xi[10] and Shen Nong[11]. Then codified for later transmission by Huang Di[12], the Yellow Emperor.

---

[10] Mythical sage of Ancient China.. Sometimes thought of as the "Creator". Established the basic skills for survival, including hunting, and communication, particularly the system of pictographs which later became characters.

[11] Another mythical sage of Ancient Chnia. He is credited with being the sage of herbal remedies and applications; as well as the great innovator in agriculture and its associated implements.

[12] The Yellow Emperor. Many classic texts are attributed to him, including classics of internal medicine and political strategy. Credited with numerous inventions and creations, including the calendar.

At first, Bao Ling balked at Sying Hao's resurrecting post standing to plague him anew. He had already had his fill of it. His well-tempered body craved the release and satisfaction of flowing and acting in the moment. He had done these punishing standing drills in the distant past alongside his grandfather. He had taken from them all he could or wanted to.

Like all young animals, he was most at home in movement. His time on the run, skirting about in the wilderness, connected him viscerally to the energies of flow. Standing like a post from dawn to mid-day. Impossible! In fact, pointless! That is, until he witnessed Sying Hao doing it with ease. Only then did Bao Ling feel compelled to reckon with his stubbornness and reluctance. He would have to come to terms with Sying Hao's challenge. *If it's important to him, it should be important to me. Heaven help us all!*

Listening Eyes

At first, and as anticipated, it proved unbearable. Sying Hao counseled, "You'd be better served quieting your mind. Release the inclination to resist." It took great discipline. Eventually the mind stilled and departed from distraction. Sying Hao then coached he must learn to "listen intently." Bao Ling tightly squinted his already closed eyes, turning his ears every which way toward sounds. Deconstructing what he took in, he tried to categorize and analyze every wisp of breeze and whatever else might be contained within. This of course set Sying Hao to laughing uncontrollably. Only to himself of course. Politeness went with discipline. Still, the spectacle proved deliciously absurd!

As Bao Ling stood in posture, Sying Hao began talking as though to himself. Or perhaps he was conversing with the tree spirits surrounding. Typically, he fretted over the hopelessness of getting Bao Ling to achieve meaningful awareness. This was not lost on Bao Ling of course, who became all the more determined.

Not one to devalue the absurd, Sying Hao ofttimes said, "We learn best by first understanding where we went wrong!" He took no immediate steps to correct Bao Ling, preferring only to monitor his practice for several weeks. Bao Ling of course felt this to be a ratcheting up of the challenge. Thus incited, he struggled to "listen" all the more intently and with unprecedented focus. In the beginning he heard nothing out of the ordinary. In time, he could discern the setting down of a bird on a branch. And on a day with clear skies, he could close his eyes and almost hear the late day movement of clouds as they lightly brushed tree tops in the surrounding hills. The delicate contact produced a wonderful, soothing hum. Bao Ling rubbed his palms trying to replicate what he heard. "Clouds?" asked his friend.

One day, Sying Hao abandoned his laughing and his comic appeals for help from the surrounding trees. Bao Ling already knew the laughing would stop when it did. Seems he had been listening and heard the thought beforehand.

Only then did Sying Hao explain how "standing like a post" and "listening" were the truest and most tried paths toward establishing one's roots. "With them as certain anchors, channels of insight opened into all the worlds about."

He apologized for not explaining sooner. Then added as justification and rationalization, "Your strained efforts at listening were simply too much fun to watch.

"Now, observe me", he said. He sunk into the classic stance of Wu Chi. Eyelids relaxing downward, his breathing slowed to near nil.

"You are now thinking, 'I've already learned it. Why are we still wasting more time with this pointless drill?'"

Bao Ling of course denied ever thinking such, though in fact he had been. Indeed, those very words had been his thoughts.

"In the tree to your right, there is a squirrel sitting on a branch, 15 chi[13] up from the surface. On the ground below, there is a toad, and to its left a rat snake approaches. Oops! Too bad for the toad, happy day for the snake. There is a hint of smoke on the wind rising from the northeast, herders setting camp. Listen, there are horses, wait, just two. But a flock of goats, no, you can't see them, you'll have to take my word they are where I say. If you look above and out to the west; that's right, over my right shoulder. High above, a crested buzzard circles intently. A hare moves behind a rock to the north. Wind pulses its fur while the tail of the buzzard flickers in interest and unison. On your left shoulder there is a wood spider. Your mind remains skeptical, but is now curious. Wait, I hear a new thought! Could it be you no longer think we're wasting time with this pointless drill?"

Bao Ling grunted. Speechless, he could think of nothing else to do. The guy was good at what he was good at.

In the days following, Sying Hao offered more on the art of listening, but not much in words really. What was there to say? Explaining and listening were two completely different arts. They did not overlap. In fact, quantifying the latter in words or structuring in thoughts only seemed to

---

[13] Approximately 1 foot. A length approximating the length of a human forearm.

make it more distant and difficult to understand, or to undertake.

Sying Hao preferred demonstrations. "Watch!" he ordered as he assumed one of the standing poses. He favored a particular five, respecting the influence of the five elements, but he did allow there were numbers of others. He shared how each master had his (or her) preferences and inclinations. In fact, it was fine to take just about any pose. He stressed how he was "standing like a post" at all times. The practice had simply become part of who he was and wound its way through everything he did. The only reason he would step into one of the postures at this stage was to set patient example for some "tortoise" to follow along. By this, of course, he meant Bao Ling.

"Take the position, then, one by one, excise all distractions from your mind. Next, remove your feelings, your opinions, your wayward thoughts. They are all needless weights, and very loud and demanding distractions. Let the weight of flesh on your limbs sink to the underside, then remove your limbs, one by one, until all which remains is the underside and your center, the dantian, heart of the underside. Then, as you find yourself lifting effortlessly over your true root, listen! Not to any one thing, but everything. Hear all directions, not with your ears, but with your dantian. Breath in what you hear through your navel, then study it within. As you breathe, you can almost smell and taste it. Not one of the five flavors, but its perfumed essence, by which all things are known. Learn to truly see! Even while eyes remain closed, thoughts alight on these experiences, opening doors of awareness and perception for your lucid exploration."

Bao Ling knew Sying Hao used words just as he shot arrows. They were carefully placed. Each word, each phrase, each sentence sailed to a specific target with unerring accuracy and uncompromising intent. He committed the instructions to memory, reciting them like a mantra until he wore them down to their dustless breath. Beneath that wind opened a new field — mirror bright, accepting all and everything at once in its sight. Bao Ling marveled like a child newly born, not knowing what to do with all he saw and felt, except simply to listen and to be patient.

In the far distance, riding streams of wind, rolling over hills and fields, slipping across the lakes, and straining up the hillside to where he stood, a voice resonated in the breeze. Perhaps that of a beautiful Fairy maiden, commemorating the moment of his first awakening.

Listening intently, the dragon
Hears the nightingale's song, the cricket's crick
A grasshopper's hop, weaving through brush thick
Swift's wings clutching wisps of air
Whispers of freedom everywhere

Eyes half closed, and root held tight
How shines this mirror dustless and right
Through listening eyes, the dragon clears his night.

Bao Ling felt the Fairy had spoken directly to him, and considered it a blessing undeserved. Though not one tempted by greed or fear to beg favors from the gods, he made exception in this one instance, before giving thanks for the moment.

"If I am deserving, please grant that I may encounter this Fairy maiden before my days are ended."

He relaxed and walked to Sying Hao who registered with a nod, acknowledging the change in Bao Ling, saying only …

"She has a splendid voice, don't you think?"

Shifting Awareness

His eyes rose again to the sign, and the words "Please be Patient."

One might argue Bao Ling was not a patient man by nature. Formed by circumstance, he had been hunted and on the run. With nothing more to lose, he became fearless, angry, and quick to react. Hard circumstance triggered his instincts for survival and forged his discipline and character. Only under the masterly guidance of Sying Hao did they achieve their final refinement.

"I can do this," he whispered to himself.

He stood motionless, appearing to hidden eyes like something carved and left for their curious inspection. From within carefully concealed view ports, warrior monks watched and studied. They mumbled to one another how he had become a statue, yet seemed to fit in perfectly. Perhaps without knowing it, Bao Ling had framed himself between portrayals of Guan Yu and Zhang Fei on both sides of the entry. Visages of the three remaining tigers Zhao Yun, Ma Chao, and Huang Zhong, stared from their own strategic vantage points alongside. It made those spying upon him quite nervous. One among them whispered to his companions, "Look how he resembles Zhao Yun! Might it be a ghost?"

They saw no breath, no movement of eyes, no tremor of ill ease, and most significantly, no thought to abandon "patience." Now it seemed, it was they who were losing patience. They had predicted he would simply leave. Why would he be different than all the others?

Bao Ling listened intently. Under Sying Hao's tutelage, he learned one could go as deep into listening as one chose — so deep in fact, the body and mind receded to the passive background, while the listening intent bloomed frontward into its own awareness. Not unlike a dream become real. In fact, even now Bao Ling wasn't entirely sure if he were awake or dreaming. Simply still, and attentive.

Sying Hao demonstrated how one might move this heightened awareness to superior vantage points. For example, hitching a ride on the consciousness of a hovering hawk, or sharing shell with a tortoise alongside a woodland trail. At first, Bao Ling thought Sying Hao had polluted his own already highly refined skills with misplaced desires for the supernatural. He said as much to his friend.

It is well known that desire and greed can poison even the best-intentioned efforts to actualize one's essential nature. For Bao Ling, Sying Hao's reports of seeing with the eyes of eagles, or roaming the deep snows on the thoughts of the great snow bears (They weren't bears by the way, but who knew what else to call them?), warranted skepticism. He made sure to provide this in abundance.

That is until one late afternoon as they prepared to
perform standing meditation to the sun's waning glow.
With what light remained on the northern horizon, Sying
Hao pointed to a white-tailed eagle. It circled high above,
apparently curious of their intentions. "Look Bao Ling, he
waits for you, and perhaps for his dinner."

Bao Ling didn't make much of it. He dismissed the
thought and set deeply into his listening state. He was after
all getting fairly good at it. Though listening, and aware of
all in the surround, his mentation had suddenly shifted. He
sensed the eagle gliding down, then flying low overhead. It
made several passes. Curiosity? At first it seemed timid.
But once assured of no threat, it circled again and called
down its greeting. Bao Ling didn't expect that. Was it
indeed a greeting? He didn't know at all what to make of it.
The call seemed inviting, almost friendly. Whatever it might
prove to be, for Bao Ling there could be no doubt. It was an
invocation rooted in the heart of wildness.

Suddenly, he felt awareness pull from his body. Then
slowly, it ascended. At first the shock of departure
registered as though something had snapped; or split in two.
Dumbstruck, he looked down and saw his body in fullness
below. He also felt his ethereal form now embarking upon
its timid first flight. Independently, it floated about.
Weightless, it lifted upward, now a vessel for his orphaned
awareness. At first, he felt clumsy, queasy, barely able to
continue. Then, by thinking to move his hands, and to stop
his legs from dangling behind like weights, his better mind
began to take over and to guide his flight. The raptor

acknowledged his first meager efforts. *Can such a beast turn and issue a smile?*

Bao Ling questioned, *Am I imagining all of this*? The eagle fluttered close by. At times its wingtips skirted so close to Bao Ling's thought body, he could feel the shift in air currents. Then it passed so near, they touched! As though with seeming encouragement, the bird's own thoughts invited, "Do what I do, follow me."

Bao Ling did as beckoned, the efforts at first sluggish and labored. The eagle circled a broad spiral and ascended. Bao Ling felt a great release within, the pull of gravity dropping from his bones and body. What was he thinking? There were no bones and body! In hardly a moment, like the wild creature alongside, he was weightless on the currents. Not sure what to do, he extended his arms and hands to the side like wings, instantly finding it wasn't required. His thoughts were all the wings needed, as well as the trailing feathers.

Suddenly he became the eagle, both of them conjoined for the moment as one. His eye, now the eagle's, surveyed the landscape, registering everything. In the impossible distance, he saw a hare being chased from its lair by a badger. Bao Ling felt the eagle's feral focus shift toward its intended meal. The raptor ascended and circled, then dropped toward earth. A challenge to the badger for its dinner trophy. Bao Ling felt the wings fold rearward and the stalker's gaze shift only to the hare, all other distractions gone from the field of view. The dive spanned more than three li. Acceleration unrestrained, Bao Ling felt the inertia of his consciousness dragging toward the rear. Fighting queasiness and struggling to shift awareness back to forward, he recovered the spectacle just as velocity peaked. *If an arrow had life, it would feel just as I do now!*

The approaching landscape closed toward them impossibly fast. In the final stages, it is as though he and the bird had become fixed and still. The surface below now raced toward them, as though to swat them from existence.

The hare flattened on impact. The badger scurried backwards, startled and caught unawares, clearly riled by this theft of a meal. The predator snared the hare with its talons. Bao Ling felt his own thoughts matching to the animation energizing its grips. The eagle instantly ascended and then hovered, as if to mock the badger. Disregarding the badger's squeals, it sought safe perch to enjoy its simple feast. Bao Ling could feel the talons severing the hare's cervical cord, ensuring its stillness. As the raptor's wings spread wide, they glided toward the tip of an ancient pine in the distance. Bao Ling became leaden with anxiety. His persisting awareness of self now overrode all and harnessed this unfolding experience to his intellect. The onerous need for analysis ripped his senses from the raptor, slamming him back into his rooted torso. Once again, he stood like a post, right where he had started.

Visually, he remained stuck somewhere between the two for some time. He fought to focus on his posture, and to quiet his thoughts, but to no avail. For the moment, he drifted and fluttered in the crack between two realms of perception. Realms which under different circumstances would never have mingled. At least not in what most consider to be our world.

Lost in the confusion, his root lifted. His consciousness dropped to the dantian, where energies of fire and water then circled madly along the governor channel until he hurled vomit. He called out to Sying Hao, "I'm dying."

"You aren't dying. It's just how these things are." At least that's what Sying Hao explained. The words brought no comfort.

"You are fortunate Bao Ling. The ability to shift consciousness and awareness is one of nature's great gifts. One, mind you, that is seldom wasted on fools. In the old days, it was a skill reserved for the Shamans. It is no easy undertaking. And, judging by the number who don't survive, we can justly conclude you have forged yourself in such a manner as to prove worthy of the gift."

"Was I really there? Could I have been imagining the whole thing? And the fury, I can't get my mind off the ferocity, or the fate of the hare, or feeling the talons sever its spinal cord as we ascended."

"Yes, you were there. No, you imagined nothing." He pointed to a massive tree on a nearby ridge. Bao Ling saw the predator perched upon its crest clutching the carcass of a hare in one talon, tearing the flesh with its beak. It looked knowingly at the two humans standing in the distance. "As to the violence, I can only say the eagle has its own way. Just as with us, it's a course determined by nature, fate, and eons of trial, test and adaptation. Violent, yes, but it falls perfectly into the tapestry of life, threading through and integrated with all which surrounds us. The eagle and the hare do what they must to survive, no more, no less. Each does to the utmost of its ability, always. Anything less, they are doomed. A time will no doubt come when even this noble bird will be rabbit for some other predator. We might both wonder if he senses that. Or if we sense the same of ourselves. But for now, that is his worry. We have our own. Never forget Bao Ling, even in the violence, the bird was swift in his kill, and in his own way, may have shown compassion."

Bao Ling thought of the talon severed spine and then the quickness of the kill. Having lived in the wild and reconnected with these inclinations within himself, he understood the dictates of survival as well as did any wild animal. Still, the differing perspective on violence, albeit justifiable, left him with more questions than answers. Perhaps foremost among them the question of what he was becoming.

Benefiting from Sying Hao's continued fostering and encouragement, Bao Ling soon enough became adept at projecting awareness. It no longer made him ill. With repetition, he grew quite comfortable with the process. During meditations, he forged new alliances for these expeditions. It became his practice to hitch rides on as many living vehicles as he could.

Yes, allies! Who would have thought? The eagle, the bear, the badger, the wolf, and many others. Each at one point or another provided shared vessel for his newest experiment. Then Bao Ling noticed something he hadn't quite planned on. Sying Hao appeared to already know all about it. Were the animals talking behind his back?

While working through the senses of his host, Bao Ling grasped it was an alliance which reached both ways. For example, an unreceptive vessel could shut the door on Bao Ling. He would be powerless to change that. But those who allowed him to enter appeared to gain something for themselves: a brief sojourn into human awareness, and its far broader scope and outreach into the ambient world. Bao Ling became more comfortable and much quicker with the projections. It was then he detected some of the creatures welcomed his intrusions. Eventually he concluded they looked forward to their own piece of the adventure, only on his turf. At times, Bao Ling even felt they had somehow told their friends. Eventually, woodland creatures could be seen hovering, crawling, and milling about wherever Bao Ling and Sying Hao might be. Could it be they anticipated the prospect they might be needed or called upon?

Sying Hao and Bao Ling both marveled at the phenomena. Sying Hao said, "The mystery of it all eludes me. It will elude you too. Be grateful. It's a gift. I don't know their motivation or their stake in this. It's just my belief nature's creatures respect an inquisitive and compassionate heart, just as they despise greed, arrogance and self-serving intrusions. Bao Ling, I have had many enemies in my time. They were so poisoned by their ambitions and ruthlessness, even the animals couldn't stand to be near them."

Part 3

Rejection Brings a Friend

Not So Crystal Springs

The temple courtyard's silence now enveloped Bao Ling as he abided by the instruction to "Please be Patient." Peripherally he noticed several snow partridges studying him from the courtyard wing to the right. There they mingled just beneath the double eaves of an adjoining stacked roof. They seemed almost tame. Probably long time residents spoiled by the largesse of those within.

Instantly, his awareness crossed to the one bird focusing most intently on the motionless human, curious and open over something new and different. The connection opened when the bird unexpectedly landed on his shoulder. The monks saw only the bird perched in presumed curiosity. A frozen in time human was, after all, an irresistible oddity. They had no clue what was about to happen.

Ascending within the vessel, Bao Ling surveyed the yard and the roof tops, noting many human eyes peering from spaces between the tiered roofs. At his respectful request, the other birds lifted and circled the compound. To his now avian eye, other monks were visible on roof tops, standing ready for the order to descend. Dressed for engagement and the call to action, they wore no robes. Clearly, the compound stood readied for uncertainty, and prepared to act. Bao Ling thought only, *Who are these monks? To what end do they maintain this fortress?*

The birds descended to the grand rooftop and sunned. Bao Ling listened. He heard footsteps within, but none directed toward the entry. He was being scrutinized, but intentionally ignored.

Respectfully leaving his host, he returned to his post standing position. The sun now high in the sky, it was mid afternoon. Much time had been wasted and lost. He would have to race the sun to get back to Zhi Mei before nightfall. He could humor his hosts no more.

Leaving his posture, he turned to the massive door, but not before using his blade to scribe new characters onto the sign. Then he confronted the door and hammer fisted a series of thunderous knocks, in long spaced succession. One after the next, the sounds reverberated throughout the compound. All but one of the snow partridges lit out, the ally standing ready if again needed.

As patiently as he stood his ground, Bao Ling was equally patient in delivering knock after knock after knock after knock, until even the surrounding hills seemed to tire of the unnatural cacophony.

Finally, the shuffling of approaching steps from within. The door swung wide. Bao Ling stared intently into the irritated scowl of a monk elder. Alongside were two disciples, presumably warrior associates judging by their staffs at ready. They would address whatever greeted or might we say, confronted him. Bao Ling knew others were ready and behind the door needing only a signal. Should it come, he'd have no escape. He knew from the partridge's scan others had already amassed at the courtyard's opposite wall.

"Do you have trouble with patience, young man?"

"Only when it tips the balance against courtesy, venerable sir."

The elder replied, "Our sign is clear young man, you failed to follow. You should leave before it grows dark. Night can be dangerous around here. If your patience is true, perhaps you'll return another time, and try again."

Bao Ling stepped back and with his hand held upward toward the sign, invited the elder, "Please Sir, show me where I have misunderstood."

The elder stepped fearlessly out, and turned about to scrutinize the sign:

"Please be Patient." Only now, he saw a second line had been etched below, "Patience folds seamlessly into timely action."

A young monk came immediately to his side, horrified at the perceived desecration, "Master, I will prepare replacement immediately, it will be up before nightfall."

The elder looked hard at the words, and remembered the guest's comment about courtesy, then turned to the younger monk. "No, I think I like this better. Let it stand as it is, to commemorate the moment."

He turned to Bao Ling, "All right young man, you have gained my attention. What brings you to our retreat?"

"I am here to see Abbot Shi-Hui Ke."

"And for what purpose might that be?" the elder asked.

For all Bao Ling knew, the man standing before him might have been Abbot Shi-Hui Ke. The wariness and caution of these monks, as well as the strategic impregnability of the temple citadel stirred a litany of questions in Bao Ling's mind as he responded. "With no disrespect intended, kind sir, my message can only be delivered to Abbot Shi-Hui Ke."

"Most unfortunate my son, Abbot is not available to meet with you, and will not be for some time. You may deliver your message to me, and I will ensure it passes to him."

Off to his right, Bao Ling's attention drew to the sound of a broom whisking over tiles. He angled his vision and saw what he thought to be an older monk, struggling with a broom. He worked feverishly knocking dust from tiles back into the adjoining landscaping. The older man was having considerable difficulty managing the broom. You see, he had only one arm. The effort might have been more than he could manage.

Bao Ling turned to the elder, "Sir, I can say only two things without breaking the confidence of my agency. What

I bring goes to Abbot Shi-Hui Ke only, and I believe he will find it serves his purpose and not mine. As to the source, it comes with the blessing of Sying Hao."

At the words "Sying Hao," a hammer of silence struck the compound. Even the sound of the whisk over the tiles froze momentarily.

The elder stared hard, "Sying Hao you say. That old ghost has been haunting Southern Mountain for some time. What might that rumored wisp of vapor have to do with you young man?"

"Sir, I have stood long in the company of Sying Hao of Southern Mountain. I have seen enough of him to assure you he is no wisp of vapor. Nor is he walking among the ancestors."

From the silence in the surround, Bao Ling felt the light rumble of murmuring voices in the air. The name Sying Hao had caused a stir, as had his answer. Its vibration rolled like vapor itself to all reaches of the citadel.

"My apologies young man, the Abbot is simply not available to meet with you. I would recommend you cross the bridge before darkness, to ensure your safety. Please do not linger, roving eyes meet untimely ends."

Bao Ling looked hard at the elder, looking for a meeting point of understanding. Nothing. In the end, he could only say, "Please kind sir, no jokes."

The elder bowed respectfully, turned about and the door shut tightly behind him.

Having been rejected, Bao Ling looked about, scanning everywhere in the courtyard. Those posted in the rear, and the spying eyes in the roof tops were gone. Only the old one-armed man remained, pacing about. Slowly and methodically, he tended to his work, paying little further attention to Bao Ling.

Seeing no other options, and regretting the failure of his task, he turned fully about and slowly made his retreat, calculating if he hurried, he might still cross the bridge before last light.

A Chance Encounter

"Young sir! Please wait!"

Bao Ling turned to see the one-armed servant waddling towards him frantically, waving his good right arm to draw attention. Bao Ling saw an aged and weathered face, wrinkled and worn by life's etchings, framed in long white hair, pulled and tied behind. His chin, naturally thin, was broadened by full mustache and goatee, white as snow, almost sparkling in the afternoon light.

"I must hurry friend. I am racing against darkness."

"I know, I know," he answered, "I heard everything. The arrogant bastards! This is supposed to be a retreat for those seeking enlightenment. No one can get in the god damned door. That should tell you something!"

"How may I serve you friend?" asked Bao Ling.

"I've waited months, months mind you, for them to go down the mountain and to the valley. I want out of here! My worn body tires of the altitude. The environment is punishing, particularly for an old invalid such as myself.

They tolerate me of course, and I try to be useful. I do the menial tasks, in exchange for scraps of food and dry cover. But continue on here? No! I have relatives in Fortune's Gateway who I pray will welcome me into their homes, feed me properly, and allow me to warm by their hearth. Anything to get me away from these hypocrites. The monks place great stock in compassion. But getting their assistance to find my relatives? No different than talking to stones."

"What are you asking of me sir?" replied Bao Ling.

"Only that I may accompany you, and if you'd be so kind as to share your food and fire, I will make myself useful and not burden your journey."

"I must be frank Grandfather. I have a companion below, who will be in jeopardy if I don't return before darkness. I fear your slow pace will throw me off the mark. Why create risk I would just as soon avoid?"

"And well I understand. Rest assured, I know these hills like my own hands. Hand, I should say. There are many cuts, passages and twists we can use to save time if you will humor my guidance. If we move steadily, I assure you we will cross the bridge with daylight. Should I prove false, simply leave me. I will not bemoan my fate."

"What of the elder's warning regarding roving eyes? Might not our using your cuts, twists and passages offend his sensitivities?"

The old man answered, "Hardly. He knows I will do what I have to do to get off the mountain, and he knows my loyalty is true. If anything, he would prefer I moved on with you, if only to keep you out of trouble."

"Perhaps you have already been tasked to that end Grandfather?" Bao ling responded.

"No my son, I do what I do, but only for the right reasons. If you help me, I will see you safely to your companion."

Bao Ling acknowledged, then apologized for not properly introducing himself to his companion, "My name is Bao Ling, of the Ling village. I welcome your company so far as to the lowland road. It is not my intention to turn toward Fortune's Gateway. In all honesty, I suspect being found in my company would only bring you unwanted trials. You are welcome to share our camp, and we will provide for you on the downhill journey, so long as you are useful. We can't carry you. When we get to the lowland road, we will part ways. I have a few imperial silvers which I can donate to your journey. Hopefully it will be enough to stay you while you find your family. Maybe when I too am old and weathered, someone will pass them back to me as I return to Ling Village."

Grandfather nodded appreciatively. Reciprocating courtesy, he answered, "Agreed. It's more than I had hoped for. I am Hui of the Shu tribes. In past times, my people lived in the mountain ranges embracing the Shu Roads. We survived by servicing the roads, and the trade. Life was hard, but rewarding, and the mountains nurtured us. They assured our survival, and kept us apart from the plagues and endless controversies of the lowlanders. Just get me to the lowland road and leave me with a coin or two. That will be enough for me to bless you for the remainder of my days."

Bao Ling turned to look Hui straight in the eye, smiled, held his right hand up for Hui to see, then hooked his forefinger and twisted his wrist palm in. The age old sign for an agreement locked. Old Hui reciprocated, bowing and smiling in return.

Never Become Regular

As they trekked along, old Hui proved quite talkative. Having overheard the conversation in the courtyard, he showed great interest in what he referred to as the "ghost Sying Hao." He wondered aloud if the Sying Hao of Bao Ling's acquaintance were one and the same as the fabled mountain spirit. Cautiously, he worked his way to asking whether Bao Ling ever wondered about falling under the influence of evil entities or fox spirits? He politely suggested if this be the situation, the alliance might not come to good end.

Bao Ling recounted the story of their first meeting[14]. Then told of Sying Hao's friendship and oversight in his growth and budding awareness. He then touched upon Sying Hao's deep knowledge of the internal arts but was careful not to say too much. To the uninitiated, what has become ordinary to those with high focus and discipline sometimes proved frightening, even sinister. He was taking no chances with the superstitious old man.

---

[14] The full account of Bao Ling's first meeting with Sying Hao is detailed in our earlier *Seed of Dragons*.

Bao Ling then turned tables and inquired into the old man's relationship with the monks. How had he ended up at the temple? Were there no other more convenient sanctuaries? Did the old man not find it strange they were so secretive and guarded? Then he pressed further, asking why he thought it was so.

Hui answered indirectly by talking of his childhood in the hills. Like his young companion, he suffered endless pangs of remorse for a once idyllic life transformed by violence and the unabated intrusion of outsiders. "Yes, Bao Ling, though you haven't said as much, in that respect, I suspect we are first cousins of fate. Our worlds might have started differently, but somehow, we've ended in the same sour stew." He laughed at the thought, then recounted the endless campaigns, and the partitioning of his own people among the interests and ambitions of warlords vying for control of the Shu Roads.

"Bao Ling," he said, "We would have been far better served had we simply ignored the jackals, disappeared, and left them to the mountains. Better yet, we should have opposed them from the moment they set foot in our hills. Resisted their every move, rejected their every persuasion, and let their corpses feed creatures more deserving than the evil spirits already consuming them from within.

"It may be a fault, but my people are compassionate by nature. Respectful, always willing to give a good listen. Ever ready to consider the merit of what you have to say. Of course, their kind see this to be ignorance — a vulnerability to be exposed and an opportunity for exploitation. When we questioned their motives and reasons, they accused us of not being patriots! Can you believe it? Patriots? Did we not care for the greatness of our nation, of our people, for our children's futures?

"What nation were they talking about? We were who we were and always had been. Didn't they know that? Did they think we were confused about this? I can't speak for everybody, but their game didn't fool me. All those mind tricks are hooks of course. Once the fish is pulled aboard, there is little hope of ever turning back. When that hook sets in your lip, you forget everything, even who you are. This they knew all too well."

Bao Ling listened respectfully. He knew these exact sentiments. He could only stare as the old man continued.

Just as with Bao Ling, old Hui also knew much more then he let on. After all, Bao Ling remained an unknown. Unproven. Not yet fully vetted and taken into confidence. In these times of new troubles brewing, trust was not a commodity carelessly extended.

Like Bao Ling, Hui had become adept in the internal arts. More than that. Within the community of monks, and among the Shu tribes, he was esteemed as a great leader, a teacher, philosopher, and healer. Mirroring Sying Hao in more ways than one, Hui had at one time been renowned as a singular archer. When the intrusions began and the mountain ways fell to the weight of change, Hui went into the wilds and resisted. Uncertain of the hearts of men, and sometimes despairing of his own people's victimization, he fought despondency by relying on himself. At least he knew who that was. He grew into manhood wandering the high ranges, making them his home, his sanctuary and refuge. In time, he became intimate with them all, and grew to know the Shu Roads as well as his own hands.

Of one thing, he said nothing to Bao Ling. As happened elsewhere, legends emerged regarding a mountain spirit who ferociously guarded the Shu ranges. The phantom toiled endlessly to frustrate the intrusions of outsiders. Him of course. His targets? Whoever sought wealth in the west, and abused the Shu and its people in seeking it. Tales and songs of young Hui's courage and uncompromising determination rippled throughout the ranges, from east to west.

Accounts of his deeds eventually wound their way to another remote enclave. There, formed as late evening campfire whispers among hunters and outcasts, they gripped the attention of a kindred spirit. None other than Sying Hao, longtime protector of Southern Mountain. Indeed, the two were marked by destiny to meet, and to become brothers in purpose.

Indeed, to Hui, it seemed lifetimes ago! The things he learned from Master Li and then from Sying Hao. If he had said anything about all that, would Bao Ling even believe it?

So, as to most of this ... Hui said nothing.

As they progressed, Bao Ling studied the old man intently. He noted one particular irregularity. What at first appeared as a heavily labored gait now waddled only occasionally. Other times, it took on the flow of a honed and adept high country trekker, almost panther like in its grace.

He figured the limp was a ruse, but why? Looking more closely to old Hui, he detected a viable and vibrant energy emerging from within, which he had not noticed earlier. It is one thing to feign incapacity hobbling about a temple courtyard. Continuing the game for several hours while descending rocky terrain will draw even the best concealment out from its cover.

"Your arm sir, would it be too forward for me to ask what happened?"

"Not at all," Hui answered, staring to his left, where the upper arm had been cut, halfway from his shoulder.

"I'm almost embarrassed to say, but one morning long ago, while wandering the highlands of Shu, I took pause to evacuate and clean myself. Until that fated day, I had the unfortunate habit of setting my weapons and implements aside when attending to my needs. I don't mean to boast, but in all fairness, at one time I was considered quite adept with the bow. Understand friend, I knew not to tempt fate. But no one's judgment is perfect. You get what I mean. When you're alone in the hills, you really think you're alone. And that's what I thought. On that one single day, I failed to check beforehand. I assumed wrong, to my great regret."

"There were others?" asked Bao Ling.

"Not just any incidental others. Can you believe it? For some reason, someone staked a king's ransom on my head. Imagine it for a moment. A man with nothing. Living alone in the wild, never even intending to leave. A threat to no one. Some aspiring council of wannabes on the other side of the eastern horizon deemed me enough of a threat to put a bounty of 500 gold sovereigns on my head. They should have offered it to me. I might have thought long and hard about taking it for my people and leaving willingly.

"Then again, probably not, priorities being what they were. Well, I was young and confident. Dangerous even! I won't lie about it. What those remote others conjured in their concerns may have been true. They knew of a young bowman roaming the high hills wreaking havoc on their efforts to reach the west. At first, they sent their officers to entice me to their cause. You tell me Bao Ling! What could they offer me to compete with the glory of home? Why, infinity passed over my head each night, and I was one with the whole of nature each day. But you know how it is. Once they're on to you, they stick to you like you know what on your sandals. More came to convince me. Then they stopped being polite and started issuing demands, then threats. Finally, they used force. It was then they felt the taste of my arrows, a bitter mouthful which suited them not.

"Well, as you know, there's no paucity of great martial artists roving the land. Most of them hungry and destitute. They have no other skills, after all. Just like everyone else, they look to and do what they must to survive. I won't judge them, neither should you. Some unprincipled ones even hitch their skills to the predator avarice of others. I'll give them this. It's true some come to understand the error of their ways. Those few eventually return to the ethic of their once masters. That's a rarity. Most are subsumed in the violence and lose themselves completely to the chase and the anticipated reward. Which of course is gone in a blink.

They are blind to all that and live only for the next bounty. In my case, I had no doubt they were already sniffing my trail. I could see the signs everywhere. There would be no more inducements to cross over, no further quarter granted.

"Of course, none were eager to take the chase into our mountains. Wisely wary, they refused to come at me individually. Always keep safety in numbers, the bounty hunter's creed. I suppose they respected my knowledge of the hills, the passes, the plank roads, the steps, the vantages, and even the shadows in the low grounds where one like me could disappear at will.

"Perhaps this will help your measure of the threat I presented. The most fearsome bounty hunters in the land eventually combined as a company of ten. Those bad boys carefully studied my history, my movements and my habits until they were able to predict and time my disadvantage.

"I tell you Bao Ling, as a friend. Never, ever become regular."

Part 4

Lost

Ten Bad Men

"In those days, to simplify the daily flow, my routines adapted to the environment. You might say, they mimicked those of the wild animals. You look like a huntsman. I'm sure you know my meaning. Without consciously minding the passage of time, you find yourself creating mental trails for ordinary tasks. Habits, which course and repeat on their own each day. They simply happen without thought or plan, hardly requiring effort. It's inherently efficient. Not unlike the wolf, whose trail to water can be mapped and timed almost to certainty.

"That was my one error. They came upon me just as I began to clean myself and had stepped no more than three paces from where I set my bow and quiver. I'm sure you know, three paces is a vast leap when dealing with demons intent on surprise."

Bao Ling nodded understandingly.

"They were upon me. So off guard, I was fighting for my life with shit still in my hands! That's what flew through my mind Bao Ling. That everything should come to naught in such a humiliating and freakish moment. Before I could act decisively, they had set upon me with silken nets, anchoring me to the ground. I was finished!

"That's what they said among themselves, 'He's finished.' So it was. They had me for the ghost. Trapped, immobile, pegged to the ground. They took their fun of course. In these times, who wouldn't? They peed, defecated, spit, kicked and stomped until they wore themselves down. Then for added measure, they set rocks upon me and assured they were burying me alive. One of them figured that wouldn't bode well for the anticipated reward. Another reminded I had to be taken alive for the bounty. Something about my knowing the mountain passes being of value to their lords. Another entered the debate, arguing it was too dangerous. All they needed was my head, and so it went until late in the evening when they tired of the debate and slept.

"Saturated with filth, and despairing of my helplessness, barely able to breathe from the weight of the rocks, I could do only what any man could do staring death in the eye. I screamed. I screamed so my agony might find wings and leave me to my fate with an accepting heart. Rage and despair; they have their moments I can assure you! Have you ever wondered how a wild animal feels when trapped? Listen, and I will tell you.

"The screaming didn't work of course. Just made it all worse. I suppose there was one benefit. It pissed off my captors. None of them slept that evening. When the midnight passed, all the animals of the wild joined in my mournful tune. I can't say why that happened Bao Ling. I can say I loved all the animals of the wild and considered them my brothers and sisters. In those days, when I paused, perhaps on the side of a stream to sun and drink, one or two of them would gather nearby, acknowledging my presence, and accepting our companionship in the wilderness. In return, I would open my sack and share what I had available to spare. I hunted, mind you. But I never took it lightly or for granted, and never disrespected my prey. I'm sure they understood that in their own way, and found I, like them, belonged to the mountains."

"And your arm?" Bao Ling asked.

"Steady young man, I'm getting around to that. I must say, those bounty hunters were real pieces of mud. Whatever heaven gave them in guile and viciousness, it took from them in brains. Next morning, they were still arguing about how to bring me back, in whole, or in pieces, alive or dead. For continued amusement they removed my rocky blanket and did their morning duties. You'd think my prone body marked center for their latrine. It could have been worse I suppose. I've heard stories of how far they'll press to dominate or to humiliate someone. No need to go there. Eventually, they agreed among themselves they could bring me back alive, so long as they kept me bound tightly in their net and slung over one of their horses. As they secured me to the mount, one of them expressed further concern regarding my history, and the stories which had spread regarding my prowess with the bow. 'What of it?' his captain asked. The other replied, 'Take no chances with this one!'

"The captain shrugged his shoulders and capitulated, answering 'Perhaps this will ease your fears.' Then he

walked to my side and gripped my left arm still inside the
net, rotating it until my hand turned toward him. With no
word or warning, he took his blade and hacked off my left
thumb. I couldn't believe it! My great skill stolen from me
in an instant! Though my eyes were nearly closed, I saw it
all, as if stuck within a nightmare. I hoped to waken and
remember every detail of their doings ... knowing so long as
there remained breath, and the ability to move thought,
there was hope. I was drained of course and had no will to
move or resist. He dropped the arm, and picked up the
thumb, holding it to my nose laughing how it smelled like a
turd.

"Well, if he wanted to capture my mind, he did. My
anger boiled over. I reached for what remained of my life
energy within and vowed the captain would someday learn
how some things just weren't funny or clever, or meant to be
made light of. As he stepped away, I had just enough
strength to slither my good hand to where it could pressure
the wound and stymie the flow of blood. Even then, I feared
the filth had already contaminated the stump.

"Bao Ling, let me say this, lest I forget. When others
oppress you and take you down, and you feel to have
reached your last thread, never abandon hope. Never
succumb. Never give up. I can attest. Karma is very fair
about these things. Should you manage, through strength of
will or other device, to survive, your day will come. I can't
say when or how, but I assure you it will. The moment will
come when you are going about your affairs, glad to be
alive, and to have survived, when you sense a slight shift in
the currents about you. Then, as you look up, you see your
once oppressors now squared in your sights. You have only

to choose whether you will or you won't, and live with the why. And, best of all, they won't have a clue of what or why when it happens.

"What the bounty hunters figured on was first to capture me, and then make their quick downhill descent to the east. They planned to backtrack their entry route. Not smart! They traveled unencumbered, with provisions for several weeks at most. By their reckoning, in two to three weeks' time, they would all be riding high with splits of fifty gold sovereigns each. Set for life!

"But, as no doubt you've already seen, these hills are alive. We have become kin to them. They've been shaped, nurtured and guided by our people from the first moment we were here. They have a mind and heart of their own, with beasts, and shadows, false passages, dead ends and mazes. For us, it's home, but for others a nightmare waiting to spring. In the deepest shadowless ravines, one might not see the sun for days, and could easily lose all trace of time and direction. The streams wind about, spiraling, and curling, sometimes seemingly uphill and circling on themselves. Mostly illusions of course, but true as the flesh on my bones. I'm sure it was the magic of the land which first drew the curiosity of the great sage Zhuge Liang. Unable to resist, he felt compelled to extract the deepest secrets from the hidden tapestries within.

"The bounty hunters mistakenly assumed they were alone in the wilderness. Funny isn't it? Seems they made the same mistake as me! My people may have been torn from their roots, and abandoned as worthless once used to the full. But they clung desperately to the one treasure which anchored them all to their noble past. One which pointed its gnarled finger to a splintered prospect of restored identity and worth. Abandoned and discarded they returned to their mountains, like children returning home. They left forever the ways of those they termed outsiders. You know Bao Ling, back then we referred to ourselves as 'the people' — not mountain people, not soldiers, or scholars, or monks. Just 'the people.' Everyone else we referred to as outsiders.

"By that we meant they were outside the realm of human experience as we knew it, and which we viewed to be the Tao's greatest gift. We would often look upon them from afar. Their leanings confused and repulsed us. We couldn't connect anything in nature with what they were about, or their disgusting habits, their insufferable arrogance, their endless opinions about everything that was none of their business, and their convoluted inclination to saddle conquest and pillage upon the backs of empty ideals.

"Having said that, I'll get to the point. To encounter ten of these outsiders penetrating our mountain sanctuary and then witnessing the desecration and humiliation of one of our own people proved too much to bear. The horror of it overcame any sense of disengagement which we might have adopted to ensure our hidden continuance."

Hui's Torment

Aimless and Lost

"The first day, as we broke camp, the bounty hunters bundled me sideways over the bareback of one of their mounts. With the constant pounding, I could hardly breathe. Less than one li into the descent, the trail appeared to split. I could hear them arguing about the fork. The marker stones they thought to have set had disappeared. They finally agreed on one direction making the most sense. Glancing carefully, I could see concern showing on their faces.

"Backtracking would not be so easy as they anticipated. Uncertainty. Perhaps you've already learned how it can gnaw at the most carefully weighed decisions. What first seemed correct proves false in its run. Their shaken confidence faded all the more when one of them noticed the water in the canyon below. Was it an illusion? It looked to be flowing westward, while they were supposed to be descending eastward. That sure tied their wits into frightened knots! The captain then tried to get bearings from the sun, but the orb was obscured by surrounding peaks. Its glow riffled off crystal formations in the encircling faces, like random fireflies floating about in shrouds of mist. I could see him blinking his eyes and shaking his head as though to clear a hallucination. He ordered they continue. They did just that, until encountering a bridge roped over a deep narrows in an adjoining ravine.

"None remembered crossing this particular span coming in. Or even seeing it for that matter. Some became visibly agitated and looked hesitatingly to me for insight. For their interest, I feigned unconsciousness. I knew the game was now underway, and I knew where it would inevitably end. My people, simple and compassionate as they were, would never think to bloody the earth needlessly. But if someone were so stupid as to become hopelessly lost in the mountains. Well, that was a different matter entirely. If their destiny had soured, and they were not of the people, the riddle belonged to them alone to solve.

"Later that day, the bounty hunters could not understand how, after crossing the bridge, and seemingly going downhill all afternoon, we ended up where we had started that morning. The horses too seemed fooled, for they hadn't even broken sweat during the re-ascent.

"My tribesmen often encountered mysteries such as this. Once, when I had just turned thirteen years, my mother sent me with some herbs to deliver to an elderly aunt. She lived in one of the downstream caves. It should have been an overnight trip, but I returned ten days later. My mother asked why I remained with auntie for so long. I told her I hadn't, that I delivered the herbs, stayed the night, then started on my return.

"'Then you had somehow gotten lost?' she asked incredulously.

"'No mother, not lost, just bewildered for a week or so,' I replied.

"That's how we learned to embrace the mountains. To love their changes, and to dance with uncertainty. We never hurried. We experienced!

"You get the point Bao Ling. By the end of the fifth day, after seemingly exploring every conceivable exit route, the rogues found themselves once again returned to their original camp. They were growing desperate.

"I certainly would have found more to enjoy in their discomfort if I weren't coming undone from the continued abuse. My arm throbbed endlessly. On the third day, the fever came, apparently wanting to explode my head. With trepidation, I removed the wrap on the hand and saw that infection had set in. Fear of the blue rot flooded my thoughts. I begged the gods for death should that be my destiny."

"Why is it always like that?" Bao Ling asked.

"Like what?"

"Well, the things they do, how they do them, why they do them? Weren't all of them once just like us. Didn't we all start out the same? I mean, happy, loved, surrounded by family, friends, community? Don't they know that when they torment you and your kind, somebody just like them is going to torment them and their kind?"

"Ah ... I see Bao Ling. You have pondered the questions of life, and like all of the ancient sages, you stand mystified," laughed old Hui. "Rest assured, you are not alone, and you stand in good company. Me included."

Bao Ling answered, "I can't say whether I ponder anything. I have no answers, only more questions. Seriously, when I catch a fish for dinner, I know why I am catching the fish, and that I need the fish, and other creatures just like him, to survive. Still when I capture him, I am taken by his wildness, his freedom plucked, and his fate stolen. Truthfully, I apologize for plundering his future, and for consuming his flesh. But I still do it. Even as I savor the cooked and tender flesh, I feel the pain of his being ripped from his home, where that very morning, the future for him seemed limitless.

"I'd like to say I am somehow different from those who tormented you, but I don't know for sure. In some ways I see that I am. But in others, I feel changes have overtaken me, and my judgment has grown cold. Like theirs. Now, it seems I see only the one or the other, and never the in-between; and I worry my compassion has chilled under my hardened eye. For me, an enemy is an enemy. If we lock in combat, I'll do what I must to survive. As to my enemy, I will either kill him or leave him behind depending on the play, and the flick of destiny. But desecrate him, maim or disfigure him? Never! Not in a thousand lifetimes! I leave my victories like funerals in my wake, and I carry the memories with me. Always! The weight grows heavier with time. I live on but wish there were a better way."

"Perhaps Bao Ling, but it is never easy for us to grasp fully and comprehend what we are not. As one ages, he learns by experience what he has become, and often hopes to be what he is not, but that is pointless. You seem to be a capable hand. And surely, your Sying Hao would not task any ordinary person to seek out the honorable Abbot. I, for one, know he can be an elusive fellow.

"Why, I'll bet you've tasted the bite of steel more than once, and that the craft evident in your well-formed arrows attests a honed warrior beneath your woodsman's tunic. Take my counsel, as from a friend. What you are serves a purpose. Be excellent at it, and never fail to show compassion; even if it starts from cold. Trust in it. It will come, if you beckon. Forgive me for saying, but it seems to this old man you are already doing that. Have no regrets for the dealings of fate or destiny's hands on the tips of arrows and edges of blades. You can't control that, all you have is what you do in the sea of circumstances, and how you do it."

Bao Ling replied, "Woods, herds, and fields shaped my youth and formed my once carefree spirit. I remember, now as if only a dream, a loving home, a nurturing community, and a bountiful surround. One day they existed, and in in another they were gone. Perhaps I've been adrift, but always, I reach to my nature as a sanctuary, and to my heritage. Warlords and their calculating minds feel they have the goods on people like us. I'm sure you get the point. They slice away everything which makes us who we are, then work ceaselessly to convert the remaining vessels into their puppet minions, existing only to serve their needs and ends.

"But resist as I might, I too have changed. Sometimes I fear it is not for the better. Not just the games my mind plays when I catch fish. I feel the pain of others when they suffer needlessly and I can't help or make a difference — because I'm alone, or because I'm limited, or because I know what I do won't matter. And then at times I move along doing nothing, with great regret and guilt. Aimless and lost."

I had Changed

Bao Ling went on, "Hoping to quiet those troubling flows within, like you I cut ties and took to the wild. Self preservation. *Leave me alone and I will leave you alone.* That's what I figured. Occasionally, their leadmen would cross my path. Some would ignore me. Good for them. Most simply couldn't resist what they felt to be another hapless target. I already possessed some solid skills from my youth, but at first, I was mostly lucky on the move. Without the luck, the skills wouldn't have been enough. You know about that, I'm sure. Unlike others who tried to accommodate and satisfice, I took my skills to heart, honed them, and in the wilderness perfected them. No choice really. Out there, it was fight to survive or perish. I survived, and eventually flourished. Others didn't, judging by their remains left to rot in the canals and fields.

"When warlords finally dispatched troops to crush the renegades, I knew they'd eventually get around to me. Because I managed to function independently and apart from the others, I became more the target. Being lucky on the move, I was able to act decisively and survive the early onslaughts. You can bet, my initial successes only complicated matters. Once they determined me to be a symbol of the opposition, I became their declared target. Rewards and bounties sprang up everywhere. Most puzzling of all, it didn't matter which warlord, or whose army. They all had it in for me. No bias there. I got the same attention from all quarters. You might say I became the fox to their chase! I'm told competing bands even made passing truces amongst themselves. Whatever it took to facilitate the joint pursuit.

"Because it was just me, only one, at first they were somewhat sporting about it. Groups of officers would be dispatched with their scouts and dogs. Together, they and their underlings would 'game' me. Hunting me as they would any wild animal.

"The day's champion, once determined, anticipated recognition and rich rewards on returning to base with my head in his hunting sack. To their eternal regret, no champions emerged. Growing numbers of promising and ambitious young officers met their untimely ends. The hunts stopped soon enough. They proved too unfavorable. Costly. Worse — an unintended embarrassment. Could it be the tables had turned? What kind of fox was this? Their own failures raised me into the symbol they had hoped to squelch. I became proof of their vulnerability. The populace could not help but to note the returning bands and their clusters of riderless steeds. Smiles could be seen shining faintly from the shadows. Not so with the overlords. When regimes rely on weight of fear and intimidation, declaring opposition futile, any chink in their armor poses grave threat to their dominance.

"So Hui, as with you, the bastards were justly dispatched by my hand. I suspect you also know this. It's a curious thing to consider. When one is oppressed or hunted like an animal, then somehow manages to survive, new skills emerge. Those skills, albeit unanticipated at first, may at times prove remarkable. The game slides off the board, as odds shift from the oppressor to favor the prey.

"Imagine … for nearly a year, nary a day passed when my life was not threatened by troops gaming me or by random encounters with renegades, brigands, and thieves. While warlords and their trustees subdued and oppressed the helpless, my skills were polishing to the highest sheen. So long as I survived, I grew stronger. It was then I found purpose.

"There's a peculiar science to it all. One might reduce it to simple repetition. Practically speaking, by the time assassins were dispatched, they were attempting something on me which they might do only on occasion. They drew motivation from hoped for reward and recognition. They didn't account for the obvious. A matter of numbers really. I defended constantly. My stakes were higher. Had they done the proper calculation, they would have seen I dealt with their kind repeatedly. For survival! Unlike them, I had no alternatives, nor room for careless error or mistakes. They had never encountered one like me.

"The struggle for survival reinforces lessons far better than any promise of reward! An infinite difference in the degree of intention! Frankly, they were no longer my match. I was simply too well schooled by experience. So, as they came, I dispatched them — coldly and methodically. And that my friend, answered for me just how I had changed. One day I had dispatched several and felt nothing! Absolutely nothing! No remorse, no pity, no sorrow. I knew they were helpless to their fate. Their unfortunate course had been drawn by others, a choreography set by their own ambitions and fears. Honestly, I had more empathy for the fish I ate for dinner."

Stirring the Mud a Bit

Old Hui nodded.

Bao Ling could see Hui had trod a similar path. Did he too struggle with what it led him to become? Or where he ended up?

"So, friend Hui, tell me how you finally managed to slip them."

"Well, the cycle continued. After day five, my compatriots elected to stir the mud a bit further. We like doing that. Stirring the mud that is. Then watching what floats to the surface. Sometimes that's all it takes to figure out what you should be doing. For the intruders, the trails they traversed no longer looked the same. Paths of once certainty vanished behind boulders, while others emerged when bushes and shadows seemed to shift. You see Bao Ling, we have lived in these mountains as far back as our collective memories reach, and what we know of their secrets is branded onto our bones. Getting lost is beyond our ability to imagine. Watching others struggle with disorientation amuses us greatly, because we have never felt so removed from our bearings.

"It was only when first encountering the cruelty of outsiders, we learned how something so ordinary and fundamental to our natures could be so effectively engaged in our defense. By days eight and nine, these ten outsiders were hopelessly lost. Not just bewildered mind you. Far beyond that point. Truly lost. Adrift and alone. For this once, they knew our hearts. Hopelessness proves a most bitter mouthful for those accustomed only to serving it out! Getting a taste of their own brew I suppose. By then, they would have been happy just to get back to the original camp. Losing the assurance of even that simple reference had set their confidence woefully adrift.

"Come day ten, their provisions thinned, and no edible prey could be found. I wondered. Had even the beasts rejected them? Their leader asked if I could get them out of the maze. My stare in response was answer enough. Then I pushed a whisper from my dried and caked throat, 'Free me and all of you will live.' That's what I told them; and that's what I meant.

"But I knew they couldn't go for that. Gold sovereigns were gold sovereigns after all. A bigger promise to them than the threat of death itself. He said he would talk with his men and come to a decision. He came back and unbound my feet then asked if I would give my word not to escape if fully unbound.

"I told him to go suck a pig's tit. Who knows whether he understood my delirious mumbling?

"He looked back to me, confirming 'I didn't think so.'

"The captain went on, 'So here's the deal. We'll unbind your legs so you can walk. I figure in three to five days, I'll know if we're free of this maze or not. We'll see how much progress we make each day. You lost your thumb on general principles. From this point, for each day we don't show real progress, you'll lose another finger. Who knows, maybe even a more personal appendage.'

"I have to give it to the guy. He really had a gift for persuasion. For my part, the infection worsened, and the tissue of the hand darkened around the original wound. We all know what that means, no need to linger on it. I prepared myself for death and waited carefully for opportunity to act. I wouldn't go out unnoticed.

"Playing along with their game, I told him I would guide them, and begged he mutilate me no further. At least I grunted something to that effect. By then I could hardly speak. He nodded his head in acceptance. That night, I stood and looked up to the heavens, constellations dancing overhead, cousin mountain dogs singing in the distant emptiness. It felt like a final embrace. With my declining strength there would be only one possible attempt. It would have to be carefully timed to the moment of first opportunity. I had hoped to take as many of them with me as possible, but seriously, I was depleted. Every few steps taken I lost balance or stumbled. I could see no easy way to secure a weapon. Nor could I even trust my hands to use one, with the net still girdling my crossed and bound arms.

"Come morning they set me to their front, then followed. It was a snail's pace, the best I could summon from my weakness. They prodded and cajoled. I knew to head for a bridge. At least there, the force might split on crossing, and when that happened, I would ride the opportunity to action. I knew just the place.

"We arrived at the roped span mid-day. To your eyes Bao Ling, it might have appeared just like the bridge you crossed today heading toward the temple sanctuary. Damned precarious wasn't it? Mind you, my people know bridges, how to build them, and how to use them. In our domain, a well-conceived bridge is always one thing above all others. A way out! We have always been outnumbered, and out armed. But our bridges, they are the great equalizer. Despite their flimsy appearance, some of our bridges have borne entire regiments and populations without issue. Liu Bei would be the first to vouch for this. But strong though they be, to my people, trained and honed in their principles and dynamics, there stands ever on each side two strands which if undone by hand, blade or ax, will unravel the entire edifice, including major cables, anchors, planks, and rails. Even more so when weighted down by traffic.

"Well, we got to the bridge. Seeing it, they were skeptical of course. Just as you were no doubt. My voice returning, I assured, in truth, they had crossed from the side of their original camp and needed to return to that side to re-establish a valid return route. Needless to say, I volunteered to go first, if that would ease their worries.

"It would have been nice, but that went nowhere. I was pulled back and two mounted scouts were sent across. Despite the group's skepticism, maybe even surprising themselves, the two made it across without issue. No problems whatsoever. I could see, things were looking up for the others, smiles of relief even opened on their lips. Then suddenly the two on the other side were calling to get the attention of their fellows. No one could hear them over the waters rushing deep below. Inexplicably, they dismounted, took lateral positions aside the bridge's track and began shooting arrows our way. At first they bounced to our front, then appeared to fall short of our end. The captain and the others were bewildered. Were they being shot at by their own comrades?

"I, for one, knew what was afoot.

"My people are what outsiders would consider an anomaly. The outsiders justify their world view with what they call 'reality.' They'd have you believe people like mine were somehow locked in ignorance and darkness. Or didn't have enough sense to make it or survive in their outside civilization. Despite this, they were sure we wanted into theirs and considered our reticence and suspicion as laziness. Or something they could tame. They just couldn't get why we didn't have drive, ambition or initiative. Probably some truth to it, happiness and contentment do lull one's judgment. You see, we considered ourselves a family, just as we considered our mountain home an extension of our persons. You might say we were intimate.

"Well, one thing for sure. We never gave up on one another. And for that reason above all others, we remained strong. Though bent and exhausted from years of abuse and oppression, we were not broken or undone. We knew who we were, and what was important, and held steady the course. At the top of that list came loyalty. You see, my people already knew I would lead my captors to a bridge, and when there, would somehow find or make an opportunity to escape. From tracks and signs they left for my studied eye, I determined there weren't enough of them to free me. But, springing a trap, most certainly.

"If you haven't surmised by now Bao Ling, one of my kinspeople spidered just beneath our feet as we were about to move forward and cross. Those on the other side saw it, and called out to warn, to no avail. They tried unsuccessfully to take her out with arrows, frankly it would have been an exceedingly difficult shot, even for me. When the Captain and those on our side realized their predicament, the captain ordered two of his men beneath the bridge to take out the intruder, then dispatched the others to side positions where they launched a crossfire.

"Distraction is a funny thing Bao Ling. You may already know this. It is very, very hard to focus on one thing when distracted by another. Then, even if you somehow manage to focus, it is even harder to think taiji and to unlock it in your awareness. You see, taiji represents the reality of movement once we emerge from wuji or emptiness and immerse in the mundane world's dance of chaos. Taiji, yin and yang, and infinite combinations of each in a spinning sphere of experience which constitutes our reality. That's the trick! How to engage it? A question answered by and known only to the few! At best, men see our chaotic flow one dimensionally, and can usually intake only the yin or the yang, rarely both. In fact, looking at the one frequently blinds them to the other. Or looking at both, frequently blinds them to the sphere itself and the realm of possibilities.

"Well practically speaking, opportunity's muse whispered to me, 'It's time!' I'd like to report I made a gallant dash through their midst, taking out whoever stood between me and freedom, and driving their steeds loose and away. Alas, I try to be an honest man in my advanced age, so I will speak the humiliating truth. I stumbled slowly away to the rear, at first backing, then turning about and stepping as quickly as my legs would follow my will. It felt like I was running in mud, no matter how much effort I expended, I barely moved.

"Yes, I expected arrows running me through with every step. Then came the great ultimate distraction. There was no other sound, just a terrifying thud. The bridge had detached completely from our side, and smashed to pieces against the far wall, accompanied by the desperate wails of two bounty hunters at first clinging beneath, then dropping to the depths below. My kinsperson of course remained secure on the near cliff's wall and would use the timeless handholds and rocky lips to spider a path to safety.

"When the remaining troops turned to take it out on me, or should I say my fingers, I was well away. Most who escape in the hills take the low path, it is quicker, and is said to offer more effective concealment. That's what they figured I did. In this instance, to throw them off, I did what they deemed unlikely. I went up. Before long, I was met by two of my compatriots who quickly guided me to an opening in the rocks. They set me safely within, carefully placing covering boulders to conceal my presence. They looked at me gravely, my left arm now black, and drooping like a dead limb on a withering tree. One handed me a knife, and told me to be patient, they would send help. I knew what the knife was for, defense certainly, compassion mostly. If they failed to return in time, fate's final decision would fall to me.

"As to the Captain and his remaining men. I had no further contact with them, as least not while they lived. I recall being in my sepulcher three days, and had only just begun to lift the blade's edge to my throat, knowing the moment had come where I could bear no more. The sound of movement outside belayed my final slice. They returned, and with them were my teachers, the only two people[15] alive who could have restored me to the living.

I lost my arm of course. It was that, or my life. The two left the decision to me. I can tell you, it did not come easy.

"Months later, after some semblance of strength returned, I made my way back to where it happened, hoping to purge my thoughts of the evil which had transpired. Bao Ling, we must never run from those things which have plagued us — another of our pesky quirks. You should take that to heart my friend. We heal best by facing them down. I stayed and wandered about for nearly a week, revisiting all the places, replaying each scene, and re-living each torment, until finally emptied of the poisoned energy. Only then could I let them slide with the mountain currents back to the sea of eternity where they would harm me no more.

"In due time my mountain friends restored the bridge, exactly as before, release points and all. You'd agree I'm

---

15 For good reason, Hui elects not to name Li Fung, or Sying Hao.

sure, why mess with perfection? As to the bounty men, they were all still there, or should I say what was left of them. Only the rocks could tell the end of their story. Perhaps in starvation and fear, they turned on one another. Or perhaps the strongest tended the weakest, who knows. I hope they were better to each other than they were to me. A pity really. In a different world, we might have been friends.

"We must never lose sight of things like that."

Part 5

Tiger Above, Dragons Below

Arriving at the Bridge

On a hilltop far from home
My friend goes on alone
Time drags a slow shadowy gait
Taunting my impatient wait

Raging water howling far below
A frail bridge invites one to know
What demons lurk and wait
Welcoming ghosts of misstepped fate

Mules stir, eyes casting fear
Quick glances all about, nothing there
I go to them hoping to assure
A caring touch, our fates now linked secure

Sounds thrash a mixed and muddled shout
Birds, creatures, water and wind
Busily tending to every whim
Here and there I bustle about

Ahead in the clouds, a fortress supreme
So far, so near, why there? A dream?
Again to the bridge, loudly down I call about

Forward and most carefully do I step out

Captured in the airy mist
Near to center, how can one alone resist
One false step, all worries be gone
What there, a wicked board tricks too timid feet
Fear, ghosts of father and brother set to greet, hang on...
too soon, too soon to embrace retreat

My friend will come this nightfall
I will be there as promised, to greet
Barely grip enough, I pull myself back
And rise more surely to my feet

Mules stir, eyes casting fear
Quick glances all about, nothing there
I go to them hoping to assure
A caring touch, all our fates now linked secure

One thing for sure. The old man proved true to his
promise. As they raced downslope against the sun, Bao Ling
found Hui could readily keep pace. The beaten down
invalid who hobbled at times like a lame duck matched the
younger step for step. Indeed, as he madly swung his
remaining arm every which way to keep balance, his feet
moved with assurance, agile as a mountain goat. He also
seemed to know every cut, path, and passage in the slopes.
He nimbly guided Bao Ling through clefts, holes and
tunnels, none visible on the previously trodden ascent. To
Bao Ling's unacquainted eyes, they sprung out of thin air.
He suspected a network created over time's long span to
accommodate the needs and agendas of those who called
these mountains home. The passing landmarks and points

of reference committed to memory on his ascent raced by. While not certain, Bao Ling reckoned old Hui's contribution to their journey likely cut return time to nearly half of what it would have taken him alone. As the sun moved into its final quadrant, the two anticipated arriving at camp well in advance of dusk.

The stories they shared helped speed their downward trek. By late afternoon, they neared final approach to the chasm, anticipating a first view of the bridge once they cleared the rocky outcrop to their front. The sun dipped over the western ridges as the two emerged from a cut between two rocky walls. There, they re-united with the foot trail dropping steeply toward the gorge. In his thoughts, Bao Ling revisited the details of Hui's ordeal. *Would I have had the same fortitude to endure and go on?* He marveled how Hui had even kept a sense of humor. There were more questions he hoped to ask, but courtesy demanded he let it rest, at least for the present.

As they commenced their final descent to the bridge, Bao Ling cautioned Hui regarding the structure and its frailty. He advised it might be better for them to cross individually. Why tempt the demons of accident and mayhem. He would feel better if Hui crossed first. Then, if there were a problem, Bao Ling would stand ready in reserve to assist.

Old Hui laughed and thanked Bao Ling for his concern. "You needn't worry about old Hui. Should death come, it would be neither the worst, nor the most dreaded of fates potentially awaiting me. I'd prefer if you crossed first good sir. If my one arm and clumsiness somehow caused the bridge to fail, or me to fall, I'd more happily depart this world knowing you would not be stuck with those sourpusses back there.

"Besides," he assured, "life is packed with uncertainty. Particularly the darkness re-emanating from the east. I would gladly welcome the serendipity of mayhem's spirits depositing me to a quieter and less labored refuge."

Considering the alternatives and stretching his jest, he pushed Bao Ling to consider yet another argument for the younger to cross first. In the event tragedy befell Bao Ling, old Hui could simply turn around and return to the temple sanctuary for a quiet but sorrowful evening meal. Perhaps marked respectfully with an offering of wine. Even as he said this, he lifted a small flacon from his pouch to prove he stood ready for all eventualities. "I would certainly miss you, young man!"

Bao Ling appreciated the friendly tender of kind humor, knowing its value. A magic spell which made seem harmless even threats of imminent danger and fatal uncertainty. Well placed jest reminded him of a finely crafted arrow. At least that's how his grandfather characterized it. He recalled the old man's words, "Properly engaged, it's sharp tip might prick the nose of an ill intent giant, backing it off for just long enough."

Keeping his mask of seriousness over the smile beneath, Bao Ling conceded, "No doubt about it then. I should go first! I would be at peace, knowing my end be so well feted."

Hui smiled and affirmed with a hook of his finger in the air.

They kept alongside the chasm to their left, first glimpse of the bridge off to their front and closing ahead. Bao Ling stood for a bit, taken in by the elaborate canvas of color and sound, all riding atop a blanket of stillness in the surround.

He listened intently. Suddenly, he began trotting forward, sensing something amiss. A faint cry of distress pushed through the rush of wind and water drawing Bao Ling's fears forward. The wail from upwind could only be Zhi Mei. Now he second guessed his decision to leave her alone, cursing his failure to give full gravity to the hazards of the surrounding wilderness.

He broke into full run. Hui, puzzled over Bao Ling's breakaway, at first hobbled behind only as assuredly as his assumed lameness would permit. In moments, his keen senses also alighted upon the subtle wail. Surrendering any further pretext, he took off like a deer following a thoroughbred, matching Bao Ling stride for stride. Not entirely surprised, Bao Ling took note of Hui's nimble trot.

They neared the bridge's mouth together. Both now saw the camp on the far side with Zhi Mei high in the rocks. The mules stood tethered behind her on the slope. Just beneath, between her and the camp below, a tiger stalked and probed. Echoes resonated from her loud screams and bone chilling screeches. Not so much fear on her part, as intimidation directed downward. She held pole and sword high over her head, hoping to create the illusion of size and prominence. What sounded like a fearful wail in the wind, now emerged to be the warning screams of a banshee. Clearly, Zhi Mei would not play the victim. The tiger scrutinized her portrayal very carefully.

The men surveyed the scene. The wary beast prowled one way then the other across her field of vision. Weighing risk against reward, it eyed the landscape for a quick path to the side or rear where it might gain advantage.

Bao Ling knew of these beasts. They were rare, and sought after by the medicine makers. Huge bounties were offered for ears, teeth, paws, tongues. Anything taken from these magnificent creatures could somehow transform into potions of longevity, health, vigor, sexual prowess, immunity, and perhaps immortality. Pretty much the standard list of justifications for any repugnant misuse of nature's treasures. In past encounters, he admired the creatures the few times they crossed paths. Their golden orange hue, accented with stripes, almost reminded him of characters or symbols. Perhaps even messages from some divine hand left to be deciphered by the Zhuge Liangs of our world. He had seen them take down bear and oxen, and knew one fully grown could easily be two to three times his own body weight.

He and Sying Hao relished the sightings. They sometimes took days from their routines just to follow about and observe the magnificent creatures. Unlike humankind, they did not kill indiscriminately. In fact, for them life was either feast or famine. They might prowl and explore for several days, barely eating and frequently ignoring available game. Almost as if their desire to hunt required a trigger to come frontward. Perhaps it was when searing heat of hunger overwhelmed whatever constraints held them back. Bao Ling often thought they were like him. They would not kill needlessly. But nature provides its own purpose. When the cat reached the point of overwhelming hunger, no prey measured too large for its need.

On one occasion, Bao Ling witnessed a tiger take down a buffalo. Trusting its instincts, it approached from the side, then angled to the rear. The buffalo had instincts of its own. Programmed by nature to find its own last opportunity for survival, it spun about, looking to sight the tiger. By then the stalker prowled low and angled decisively.

Surely the buffalo could sense the outrageously bright colors and stripes against the placid surround. But not. Even Bao Ling's trained and impeccable eye suddenly lost the beast. "There it is" whispered Sying Hao. "Where?" asked an incredulous Bao Ling. Sying Hao pointed to movement in the tips of wild grass alongside, observing, "Remarkable isn't it. His radiant array of color suddenly blends in completely with the bland surface growth."

Once confident of the kill to be, the beast crawl-stepped at first, then finally accelerated obliquely toward the buffalo. Sensing movement only at the last instant, the prey kicked hard to its rear, catching perhaps a glancing blow to the tiger's side. By then, the cat was airborne. Before the buffalo could move again, the cat landed four point onto its back. Front paws quickly locked round the bovine neck, claws now throat-embedded and teeth already ripping through flesh, muscle and arteries.

The buffalo flailed and howled. Sying Hao looked and studied impassively. Bao Ling at first turned away. Then accepted what must be, giving due respect to the courage and skill of the tiger, and to the sacrifice of the buffalo. It was not lost on Bao Ling how the cat feasted for some time. Famished, it downed perhaps a quarter of the buffalo before abandoning remnants to the vultures and other scavengers lingering patiently nearby.

The two watched silently, until the quiet was finally broken by Sying Hao. "Bao Ling, always remember. You and the tiger are brothers. Within you grows the same hunger. For now, you have tabled your appetite, but the time will come and you will know it. It will be for you to decide how and when it must be sated."

Taming the Tiger

They arrived together at the bridge, then stopped. No time to lose. Bao Ling already had bow in hand as he screamed over the sound of the waters raging below, "Don't move Zhi Mei! Be still! Don't even breathe!"

She saw him. Her questioning look told she didn't hear a word he said.

He set his arrow then readied. Figuring distance, he estimated just over half li. Gauging wind, he looked for signs of meddling gusts and invisible currents. Next he studied the bridge and its cables for drift, then scanned for birds in flight. How they compensated would tell much about shifting breezes. Satisfied at last, he set. Old Hui whispered over his shoulder, "You'll need to mark further left to hit the tiger."

"I'm trying to spare the creature. Besides, who can say if striking the beast with a shot from here will have the momentum to take it down. Injured, its instincts might just make it more lethal. I'm gaming a well placed shaft will startle it. With luck, it will disengage until we cross."

Hui nodded in approval, then stepped back to clear the shot. He readied Bao Ling's quiver for quick follow-up if necessary.

Zhi Mei saw him reckoning and knew what to do without being told. Once satisfied she had stilled, Bao Ling took careful aim, then released his first shot. It arched gracefully over the emptiness and dropped to the rocks separating the beast from Zhi Mei.

Startled by the unexpected interference, the animal spun immediately about to check for unwanted intruders. Then, to assure itself, it paced warily, first one side, then the other, until it had scanned all directions and reckoned no immediate threat.

Assured by the shaft's trajectory, Bao Ling unleashed five more, each closing more threateningly from where Zhi Mei stood, downward to the animal's position. The last arrow, a blunt end shaft, glanced off the animal's right shoulder.

The clearly annoyed beast now jumped back. Sensing something amiss, it stalled to re-assess its intentions. Zhi Mei added her own menacing glare to its uncertainty of the moment. Her valiant effort perhaps to no effect. What the beast saw in her glare could not offset what it read in her body's involuntary tremor. Among creatures of the wild, as with men, this proclaimed vulnerability.

You see, of all nature's wild creatures, cats rank most methodical. They calculate carefully. They survive in the wild only so long as they are successful predators. Their hunting instincts have been polished and honed free of nonessentials by long evolution, and then perfected in their use. What cats lack in endurance, they compensate for with stealth, and the ability to move quietly. Typically, they feed once weekly. On average, their prey will be less than half their size and weight. Once caught, most victims will be devoured in one grand feast.

They prefer hunting at night but can be tempted to strike in daylight should opportunity justify. Among the great ones, their majestic and flamboyant colorations would scarcely be expected to provide cover. Such thinking on anyone's part would prove remiss. Tigers will rarely be seen until they have come upon you. The few woodsmen or travelers lucky enough to have survived relate how they were nearly eye to eye with the beast before even knowing it was there. Great cats prefer to attack from the rear and can move so quietly as to be unnoticed. Typically, they will rip their prey's throat and blood vessels from behind. An operation well underway before their target's first thought of resistance.

You understand, a tiger can't afford to be injured. Being kicked or butted, or gored by a horn might spell death. Being the methodical strategists they are, their every move minimizes exposures to such risks. Should they fail in this, any injury of consequence takes the edge off their hunt. Without that edge, they quickly down spiral to starvation. They are well practiced at what they do. In a typical year, they may attack as many as fifty sizable prey. They stalk cautiously. Where the shock of attack fails, or brings on too much risk, they'll disengage, rather than incur disabling injury. Better hungry for the moment, than lamed.

This particular animal first came upon Zhi Mei from her rear. As it stealthily approached, she sensed something amiss from the movement and nervousness of the mules. The tiger expected her to run and would have come on her from the rear. She didn't. That probably saved her life. She turned, removed a hollow bamboo tube from her satchel, and shot bird darts toward the beast. That ploy stopped its death march cold. Puzzled by this threat, and concerned for its delicate eyes, the tiger moved gingerly forward as Zhi Mei backstepped to the mules. The tiger knew it wanted no part of a mule's kick, though it still hungered for Zhi Mei. Such became the tiger's dilemma, the long pause buying time for Bao Ling's return.

That remained the scene when he and Hui first heard the cries.

Now taken by this second imposition, the animal carefully regarded its designs, mapping all prospects. Anxiously, it paced about, weighing its hunger versus its trepidation to nudge further against the unknown. It circled to its rear, scanning and scenting in widening arcs, suspecting threat and danger, but knowing only one thing for certain. The delicate creature above continued her shiver of fear, a beckoning too irresistible to ignore. Bao Ling and Hui seized this pause to quickly begin their crossing. Still in motion, Bao Ling lifted a killing tipped shaft to his bow, yet held at the ready for what hopefully would not unfold.

The cat caught the quick movement of their approach and read their determination. It saw the two men as secondary predators, like dholes[16] or vultures. Intent on seeing what they might harvest from the anticipated kill. Staring at them intently, it carefully considered their presence, finally determining they posed no immediate threat.

As they neared span's center, Bao Ling sensed the subtle and capricious drift of the bridge. He knew it would reduce the promise of a shot from sure, to uncertain. Frantic, he abandoned all caution and accelerated, hollering loudly and gesturing wildly to draw the cat's attention.

But the cat was no fool. Nor would it allow any secondary predator to steal first rights to this dinner. In its mind, but for the capture, the prey was all but taken. The cat darted quickly toward the bridge, glared and sounded its warning to back the intruders. To the cat, they seemed just like the one above: insignificant vulnerable creatures.

Except the two on the bridge issued no tremor and gave no sign of fear. Leaving no doubt whose turf they were on; it then trotted a wide arc casting its final dare. Concerns resolved and sensing need for immediacy, it turned to gallop obliquely uphill. All attention returned to Zhi Mei. Not yet across, Bao Ling drew his bow for the killing shot, but struggled against the oscillating structure beneath. Only one shot. One chance. Zhi Mei immediately realized the predicament. She stood tall, again raised her props, then attempted to reposition amongst the mules. Bao Ling,

---

[16] A type of wild dog common to Asia. Fierce hunters, known to have engaged tigers. They are an ancient species among the canids and have been memorialized in the writings of Rudyard Kipling (*Red Dog*).

horrified at this script now spinning wildly out of control, eased his draw on the bow, and called to Hui, "She's lost, unless I can get to ground first!" Hui acknowledged with a nod, and Bao Ling accelerated to bridge's end, racing death to the line.

Wasting no time, the beast cut the angle, then sprinted to the final kill. Bao Ling flew from the bridge and readied just as the cat prepared to go airborne and finish its dire task. No longer shaking, Zhi Mei stood gallantly, her firm stance giving base to a sword held forward by two steady hands like a fang threatening to her front.

Finally set solid on ground, the archer drew his bow for the kill.

He was too late!

In shock, Bao Ling stood paralyzed expecting only to witness the consequences of his earlier misjudgment. She should not have been left alone!

Just as death readied to leap the threshold, the beast appeared to have been rammed from the side. Its airborne torso lost course, spiraling awkwardly off into space.

The now terrified animal somehow managed to land on its feet but wanted nothing further to do with any of this. In a golden blur, the brute cut downhill and away, effortlessly disappearing into the encroaching darkness.

Puzzled over this miraculous development, and knowing he had nothing to do with it, Bao Ling turned to Hui. He found him still on the bridge. Still locked in a forward bow stance, left foot to the front, right hand behind the ear, fingers spread open confirming the release. The ghost of his left arm lifted up and forward by what remained of his shoulder. Its invisible grip anchored a phantom bow. All framed by his deeply set eyes locked in utmost focus, confirming what one master archer recognized to be the perfect shot of another master archer. Only no bow, no arrow, no arm.

Hui immediately relaxed, then hurried across the bridge to Bao Ling's side.

Bao Ling looked to him in earnest, "You know, that's some arrow you just shot."

Hui nodded, "Yup."

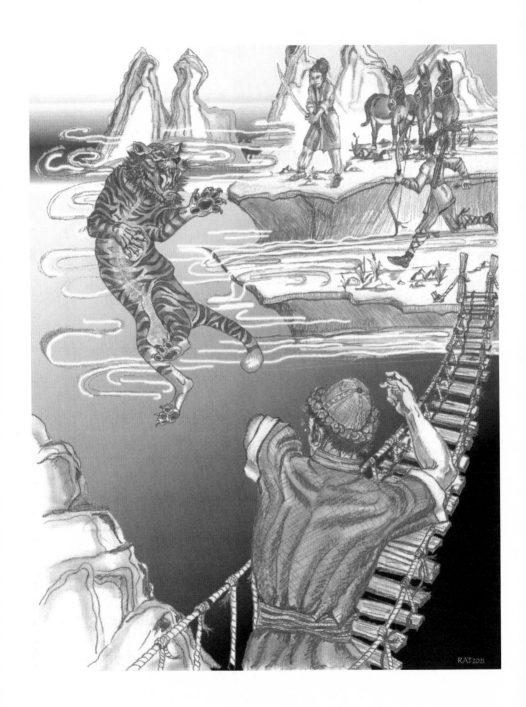

Abbot Shi-Hui Ke

Zhi Mei jumped from her rock and ran to Bao Ling, who closed from the opposite direction.

Suddenly bridled by reticence, both stopped, barely arm's distance apart. Old Hui saw their dilemma immediately.

Bao Ling, searching desperately for the right words, mumbled, "Are the mules safe?"

From where he stood, old Hui winced as though stung by a bee.

Zhi Mei, surprised at this turn, snapped, "Of course the mules are safe. I was watching them. Didn't you notice, I had the tiger at bay until you almost impaled me with your arrows!"

Bao Ling's puzzled expression punctuated his own awkwardness. For him, a most unfamiliar circumstance. Restraint be damned, he stepped forward, reaching his arms around her, and pulled her into close embrace. Picking his words more carefully, he spoke to the top of her still sun-scented hair, "True, but real friends still worry. Even when everything appears to be almost under control."

With hands on her shoulders, he held her out to arms' length and simply stared into her eyes, catching the sun's nearly quieted golden glow still lighting the pure beauty of her indomitable spirit.

Soon enough, old Hui joined them, making sure to re-establish his marked limp. The effort proved of no point. Not knowing all which had transpired beforehand, and assuming the obvious, Zhi Mei turned to the old man. She thanked him for his timely intervention, then introduced, "I am Zhi Mei, of Mei village, most pleased and humbled to make the acquaintance of the eminent Abbot Shi-Hui Ke."

Bao Ling, about to interrupt and correct, deferred to old Hui, who responded to Zhi Mei, "At your service and most honored to make your acquaintance young lady. I have long been charmed by the songs and verses lifted to the winds on the wings of Mei Village's nightingale. A family of poet farmers in such times as ours. A great rarity, and a blessing. And my condolences young lady. Even here in the mountains, we know of, and grieve your tragic loss."

As he heard the words, Bao Ling saw years drop away from the old man. The once bent from age lumbering cripple abruptly transformed into a vibrant man of middle years. Even the skin tone lost its ghastly gray tint. Bao Ling could scarcely believe his eyes. He looked carefully, almost expecting to see the left arm back in place. He knew of Colonel Sun's mastery of the transformations[17] from Sying

Hao, and to a degree had witnessed Sying Hao's wizardry. But this staggered the imagination.

The Abbot turned to Bao Ling as though to explain more but added nothing. "More courtesies later, we must move quickly with what light remains. Gather your things, prepare the animals. We return to the temple."

Bao Ling started to object to any bridge crossing involving Zhi Mei and the animals. Before he could protest, Abbot Hui pointed up stream drawing Bao Ling's attention to the movement of others approaching. They appeared to float up from the ravine itself as if riding on the backs of clouds.

Frontmost appeared to be the elder he had met earlier, accompanied by other monks from the sanctuary. The purpose in their movement showed their routine to be well choreographed and oft repeated. In short time, they met in silence and their combined caravan quickly assembled. The old one guided the troop upstream, high alongside the narrowing corridor walls. But now, Bao Ling noticed something new. The ambient sound had somehow lifted. Where earlier the water had raged below, now he heard only a faint murmur. He stepped to trail's edge and peered into the depths to see what had changed.

---

[17] In the Legend of Monkey King, Sun was granted mastery of the 72 Transformations by his teacher. In effect, he had the power to shift shapes at will. Except for his tail, which could always be found, if one knew where to look.

In disbelief, he discovered the torrent had nearly
stopped. Abbot Hui came alongside and said, "Zhuge Liang
may be gone, but his guiding hand remains. As you may
have gathered, the temple sits isolated, protected on all sides
by cuts, and deep ravines. When Zhuge Liang and his
brothers Guan Yu and Zhang Fei first scouted the range,
they found an endless maze of trails, paths, perilous ascents,
confidence shaking river crossings and spidery bridges.
Zhuge Liang, above all others, understood the importance of
controlling the Shu Roads and the many mountain passes, as
well as the waters beneath. He devised a system which, if
ever challenged, would grind the determination of any
threatening force to impotence. The three of them loved our
mountains, and our people came to love them, eventually
accepting them as revered elders. They had our hearts and
our trust. Much of this preceded my time of course. When I
first took to the hills as a youth, a system had already been
conceived and the implementation begun.

"You see, like the natives, Lord Zhuge and his
companions saw our mountains as alive with purpose. If
properly readied, they would provide an impenetrable
barrier against invaders who otherwise saw them only as a
direct line from east to west. At the first, they naturally
shielded Liu Bei's escaping forces, closing his rear to threats
from the south and the east. The only viable alternative for
the pursuing armies was the far north, which had untenable
disadvantages of its own. For Cao Cao to attack from the
north would take time and great expenditure of resources.
The supply lines and their logistics would be stretched to
unprecedented lengths. There would be considerable
resistance from the nomad horsemen along the way. The
tribes of the barren north wanted no outsiders crossing their

lands or stealing their cattle. Worst above all, any opportunity for surprising Liu Bei would be lost in the delay of approach.

"As the situation stood, Lord Liu's army had already been depleted by Cao's ruthless onslaught. His western kingdom had not yet taken shape. What limited forces he could spare would scarcely stall invasion from the north. But from the east, he remained especially vulnerable. He knew the greater force would have to be deployed against any onslaught from their rear. Lord Cao would direct his legion to pursue them westward, directly into the Shu Mountains. No doubt, he counted on the mountains to grind Liu's front, while he cut away at the rear. He called it the "Use Tail to Pull Tongue Strategy."

In the end, Liu Bei wisely sent Zhuge Liang, Guan Yu and Zhang Fei to find a solution. In those days, elders said that Guan Yu and Zhang Fei each represented the equivalent of ten thousand experienced warriors on the battlefield. But Zhuge Liang, he was like an army of ghosts. They would explain, "You might see only a single man, no reason to fear or feel threatened. But when he moved about, entire battlefields fell into chaos and disarray. Many, certain of victory going in, ended humiliated in utter defeat, barely able to escape with the tails of their fleeing horses." But all of this came before Liu and his companions achieved their glory days. At first, they were like anyone else on the run.

Bao Ling looked closely at Abbot Hui, still parsing how the old man he befriended had been a complete charade. And wondering why? Bao Ling stood true; he was who he was. He had no place for laxity or tolerance when others failed that same measure. His skeptical look to Abbot Hui marked his discomfort. Had anything been real in what they shared? To what degree had it been mere baiting? His discomfort at being played grew evident.

Abbot Hui paused and stared, "Ah, Bao Ling. I can see your quandary. You feel I have been dishonest with you. Perhaps that I took advantage of your trusting nature?

"My deepest apologies my new friend. Here, humor me for a moment. I propose we begin anew. I will work to earn and deserve your trust, and that is as it should be. In these times, nothing stands true, unless first tested. You have already met my test and passed."

Bao Ling focused on Hui's eyes, "But, of all the things you said, what is true? If anything? You do understand, deception is more often the stock of scoundrels."

Taken aback by Bao Ling's response, Abbot Hui countered, "Yes, Bao Ling. I deserve that. I too have tasted your struggle with what becomes of us once we adapt our own behaviors to counter those of our oppressors. How about this as a first step. Before I assumed the role of Abbot, I was Hui of the mountain people. Since I consider you my friend and comrade, I will always be 'Hui' to you, just as I am to my own tribe. And as with them, and Guan Yu, Zhang Fei, and Zhuge Liang, we will stand as brothers against whoever preys upon the innocent."

Bao Ling looked hard at Abbot Hui, tumblers seeking rest points in his concerns. He recalled how Hui's "thought arrow" had cast the balance their way earlier when all hope seemed lost. On that point, he and Zhi Mei remained in Hui's debt. Opting in the moment to trust, he smiled, then added, "Agreed, provided you tell me the rest of your story, and your nearly complete return from Yama's doorstep."

Dragons Below the Surface

"Nearly complete return?" This puzzled Hui, until he reflected, then looked to where his arm had once been. "Ah, humor as an after dish to near disaster. Rest assured. I intend to cheat Yama even more before my final stumble across his threshold."

He took Bao Ling by the arm and instructed they remain together. There was yet something else he wished to share.

The party stepped carefully over the ravine's edge to an otherwise unmarked and undetectable trail. It led downward, like a finger scrape in the wall, angling far below to the base. There was scarcely space between wall's edge and the drop to a now far reduced stream. Had the torrent been at normal level, they might already have been swept to oblivion. Hui began telling his friend about Zhuge Liang, this time tying his words to what lay ahead.

"Nearly from the first, Zhuge Liang knew the Shu Roads would be the key to their ultimate survival, and to their eventual return to strength. He called the insight one of the great awarenesses of his life. Leaving nothing to chance or speculation, he and his companions walked and explored for nearly a year. Over the course of many trips and studies they carefully documented all they discovered. Certainly it had been dangerous for them. They skirmished frequently with probing forces from the east. In some instances, full battalions. But what can you say? In Guan Yu and Zhang Fei, Zhuge Liang could have no finer guarantors of his safety and purpose.

"It's a fact, as no doubt you've heard. Guan Yu was renowned for his sense of propriety and righteousness. He forever protected the weak and vulnerable from those who sought to disadvantage them. As they roamed our hills, it is said Guan Yu left his brothers frequently. He needed to know. To scout and learn for himself how the incoming marauders tormented the indigenous folk. He had heard the accounts and the reports. But what he heard wasn't enough. He had to see with his own eyes. Wherever he went, he impressed. Among my people, stories abound of his miraculous interventions, and of the fear he struck in the hearts of would-be oppressors. Eventually those scoundrels knew to march past any village or homestead fronted by a shrine soliciting Guan's protection.

"As to Zhuge Liang, nothing escaped his insight. He knew, should our people fall, the west would be split wide to invasion and rapacious exploitation. He would have none of that! He had to figure a way to close Liu Bei's vulnerable rear. And, at the same time, free forces to shield against invasion from the northern front. A key element of this strategy was emboldening the mountain people. He would unloose them to survive using their own initiative, and whatever advantages he could impart to them. Somewhere in all of this would arise a convergence of purpose. A grand alliance. No doubt about it, he was the man for the job!

"We knew of bridges and their principles long before any others first came. We built them and maintained them for ages. Zhuge Liang understood just how important they would become to our mutual security. It was he who taught our elders how to make bridges as sturdy as the mountains beneath but still able to melt away whenever escape or survival demanded. This was no ordinary scholar. He had dirt under his fingernails and the calloused hands of a mountaineer. We trusted him completely, and our trust proved well placed. Our contract with him stands even to this day. It saddens us deeply he is long gone. His spirit imbues these mountains and will be here until they've turned to dust."

By this time, stars sparkled overhead like luminous crystals, seemingly held aloft by the walls surrounding. Only a distant afterglow lingered from the day. The group assembled at water's edge, then crossed in single line. They stepped carefully onto rocks placed long before as footholds in water barely touching thighs. Scanning the surround, Bao Ling could barely make out water lines along the adjoining walls. They showed levels many times his height, still wet and discolored from the day's earlier flow. He looked further upstream and in the distance saw a fall of water, dropping majestically from heights above. He determined the volume to be many times what he saw before him. The waterfall appeared to be one of several feeding the flow. Nothing he surveyed accounted for why it reduced so dramatically to what little remained where they stood.

He turned to Hui, "I have a question."

"Ask."

Bao Ling continued, "Earlier today, the river ran as a raging torrent. Uncrossable. The only path appeared to be the bridge, but even that seemed suspect."

"And your instincts were true Bao Ling. You knew to leave the mules and your companion safely behind. That was smart. Doing otherwise would have been dangerous. But I'm curious, what did your cautious eye tell you when you first surveyed our sanctuary."

Bao Ling answered, "From Sying Hao, I had already learned of Zhuge Liang's brilliance and of his hand in the destinies of others. I knew of his wanderings in the high country. Particularly his efforts to seal tightly the Shu Roads from those who threatened the rear of Liu Bei's retreating forces. I saw the ravine, and the bridge. When I looked across to survey the terrain, I saw how it framed the temple's well protected footprint. I recognized it to be a fortress impenetrable. So brilliantly conceived, it belittled any pre-imaginings. In practical effect, it amounted to a stronghold surrounded and secured by canyons, cliffs, raging streams and narrow passages through rocky faces. Accessed by bridges only the most fearless would venture to cross. And then only after considering their vulnerability to archers who might already be guarding the intended end. In effect, for the first time, I knew for my own self the very thing Sying Hao had so often told of: the undeniable manifestation of Zhuge Liang's genius. Truthfully, in that moment, I felt Sying Hao had not done him proper justice with his frequent praise.

"Still, for me, the mystery lingers. This river raged uncontrollably earlier today. Now, it appears to have been tamed. How so?"

Abbot Hui tugged Bao Ling's sleeve and whispered, "Follow me."

After crossing over, Hui directed the monks to lead the procession escorting Zhi Mei up to the temple compound. Accommodations were already underway for their anticipated stay. Bao Ling, knowing he would be alone with Hui, secured his pouch and returned to the monk. After watching their companions disappear into the rocks, Bao Ling turned to Abbot Hui and asked, "Where to now?"

Hui left the trail and angled toward three huge boulders. They stood like elephantine guards before a fissure in the rock face behind. As they neared, Hui reached back and threw a handful of pebbles at the wall. Bao Ling figured the sound alerted someone nearby. Then, to his astonishment, the fissure slid open, revealing it to be two mammoth slabs. They rolled almost frictionlessly, barely audible. Guided from beneath and above along tracks carved and set by hands from another time. Stepping through, the two were immediately met by warrior monks, forewarned and on the ready. Just like the bridge, and the trail to the river bed, the doorway accommodated only one person passing at a time. A handful of guards could easily defend the corridor within.

Bao Ling's eyes adjusted to the light of torches which lined a path downward through one of what appeared to be many tunnels and passageways.

Hui assessed Bao Ling's amazement, noting "The river is Zhuge Liang's trick. So too is the door — actually but one of many more. Just like our bridges. Functional, efficient, sturdy, but capable of instant collapse, should the need to escape arise. The tunnels were nature's gift, though honed to further perfection by the cleverness of Zhuge Liang.

"You see, our hills are ancient, as are the evolving flows of our great rivers and watersheds throughout the range. Over eons, water's ceaseless carving has shaped every inch above. But the dragon spirit governing flow of waters also masters that which lies beneath. Few know this. The very same streams which rage above. You've seen how they seem randomly to appear and disappear into and out of the cliffs, caves, tunnels and falls. They have carved their own networks here. Like blood vessels within the mountains. These passages and flows easily rival the Shu Roads above. Even our people were unaware of this once unseen domain — until Zhuge and his companions started disappearing inexplicably into the ground. Days or even weeks would pass before they surfaced to rejoin us as "ghosts." In some cases, long after we had already held their funerals and memorials. At first we mountain folks didn't find it humorous, but before long, we were pulling the same stunts on each other.

Part 6

No More Secrets

Delivered as Promised

"Honestly, for warriors who could strike someone dead with a glance, or a spell; these were three very hilarious fellows.

"You may not know this Bao Ling. It was our people who crowned Zhuge Liang with the title 'Sleeping Dragon.' You see, everyone would underestimate him. To us, he looked like any one of us, and could have been the man from one village over. A regular fellow.

"That, more than anything, made his true nature all the more compelling. He coursed through reality with the authority of a dragon. Intelligent, gentle, compassionate, loyal, friendly, great musician and poet, strategist supreme, wizard, the list never ends. He needed none of us, nor did he need the nonsense brought by the dregs of mankind into this world. I almost said his world. Indeed, not his. But he stayed; and he stuck it out. I give him credit for that. I like to think he had his reasons, but I can't fathom what they might have been. So, just between you and me, I decided for myself what it was.

"Compassion! The man radiated compassion. Some argue he did it for riches, honors, power, recognition, and prestige. Ridiculous! He cared not a whit for those things. It was compassion. Some of the ancients who knew him often told of how he would very systematically feed the birds, and lay crumbs out for the insects after his meals. He couldn't pass a beggar or a leper without stopping and learning more about them and what brought them to their state. Then seeking some way to ease their burden. Sometimes even concocting a miraculous cure. Yes, he loved Liu Bei, and remained loyal until the very end. But when it came to compassion, he was the dragon, not Liu Bei. Believe me when I say this. Without Zhuge Liang, Liu Bei, Guan Yu, and Zhang Fei would be known today as just another band of misguided firebrands.

"Well, it was Zhuge who appreciated the significance of our caves and our tunnels. It was also he who braved the darkness, mapping the subterranean passages, and the flows of waters within. In time, he determined the combined attributes of the surface terrain, and the hidden corridors below allowed for the creation of unassailable fortresses at key locations. These defined forever the boundaries of the Shu Roads. And best above all, there are fine temples to boot."

"And Crystal Springs Temple is one of those fortresses?"

"Most certainly; 'temples' if you will!"

"But we come again to the water, how is it possible to still its flow."

Hui smiled, then continued, "Ah, the magic of it all. It didn't take long for Zhuge Liang to conjure methods for manipulating the waters coursing below. Devising locks, and networks of gates, he actualized the science of controlling water's flow at will. Diverting it to unseen reservoirs, then returning it elsewhere downstream to its natural course. In the case of our river outside, it is fed from sources in the high eastern country and drains in the lowlands to the south. Zhuge Liang's system of locks and side channels exists within the mountain, subject to our manipulation. What you saw today involved our draining the water upstream, diverting it through tunnels and channels, and letting it release back into the river in faux falls below. Now that we've all crossed, my fellows will restore the channel, and re-gate the underground tributary, allowing the surface stream to again rage impassable."

The two remained below for some time, with Bao Ling studying the network of diversions, and the systems of wheels, pulleys, levers and gates making it all possible. He wondered how anyone could intuit such intricacies, then will them into reality.

They eventually returned to the surface. The mountain evening cooled, and the planets trailed across the sky. Intermittent clouds of bats flittered curiously above the two. In the distance, wild mountain dogs called their soulful medleys.

They arrived at the compound, cooled enough from their long trek to welcome the fire blazing within. There they sat about for some time and did what common folk enjoyed most. They traded stories.

Allowing their privacy, the others retired to their chambers, and only Hui, Bao Ling and Zhi Mei remained.

It was then Hui turned to Bao Ling, "Now I have a question for you. We are alone, and you can speak freely. What errand are you running for Sying Hao? How am I involved?"

Bao Ling scanned the surround to ensure only Shi-Hui Ke would hear. Once assured, he looked to Abbot Hui saying nothing, lest even his whispers be caught. He lifted the pouch and set it before the Abbot.

Balancing it against his leg, Hui removed the ties, flipped the cover, and opened the protective skin within, taking full account of the accumulated treasure. He looked back to Bao Ling and Zhi Mei, nodded somberly, then asked, "And what instructions did Sying Hao give?"

"He said you would know his mind."

Hui smiled, "Of course, what else would he say."

Then he whispered, "Bao Ling, this represents a princely treasure. Did you know what you were carrying?"

"Of course, that's why he had me carry it. He would have preferred coming himself, but it was not possible."

"Ah, no doubt, the Southlands," Hui mused.

This surprised Bao Ling, *How would he know that?*

Hui continued, "Having the pouch before me, I confess that lingering wails of suffering and pain call out from within its folds. Even as I sit here with you, my heart and awareness are delivered to the cost of this sour harvest."

"Yes" Bao Ling added, "I know what you're saying. I am glad to be rid of the weight."

Hands Are Last to Go

Shi-Hui Ke mused on his words, then answered, "Yes ... the weight! We teach how compassion and empathy bring heightened awareness to those who cultivate the traits. I suspect you know what I mean. Is it a good thing? A true gift? Who can say? Those in power regard this art as a sure sign of weakness. An unwanted departure from ruthlessness.

"The warlords and their bands can do what they do because these virtues have been excised from their characters. To capture the spirits of others, they must first work the wicked chicanery upon themselves. They are well rehearsed and know from themselves how to make this happen to you. More skilled than physicians, they take what has long been within you, and ruthlessly purge it, leaving only an empty shell. This they fill with their message, pouring in garbage until the vessel flows over, and can hold nothing more. They control that message, and in time, steal your very thoughts.

"If they don't get to you first, then it will be your children, or their children afterward. Eventually though, it gets done. Once they have your mind, they go for your legs.

Before you know it, you're doing their dance. You gather where they want you to gather. You move where they want you to move. You remain still where they want you to remain still. Eventually you march to where they send you. By that point, you belong to them. There's no turning around and finding your own way back.

"It's your hands that are different! They are the hardest for others to turn. Who would have thought? You see, you can be made to walk evil, to think evil, to speak evil. You may even be taught to want evil. The great leap though is to the hands. Try getting them to do the dastardly deeds. That's where the wheel binds to the road. They will not give in so easily as the rest of you.

"Right in the moment when you think your heart has hardened completely to stone, and you are about to use or take your first innocent. You will find to your bewilderment the compassion and empathy long deemed purged, have taken refuge in your hands. It only makes sense. It is after all those two that have to do the dirty work. The warlord may devise the plan and pull your strings. You'll buy into what you are told you must do, and lust after the promised payoff. You really won't have a choice, will you? Your feet will walk you right up to the executioner's boots. Just step in and pick up the hatchet. It's as though they were made for you. But your hands, they'll bear the true weight of action. They'll want no part of the evil blade or its purpose. Just as you are about to unleash the decreed torment, the hands will stall. They will question your purpose, and your heart, then demand you stand in the shoes of the intended. Like a stern parent forcing your third eye to turn inward and see evil for what it is.

"The one true view rising above all others. You will see yourself through the eyes of the oppressed. It's compassion's greatest gift, and the only way back. So, even though you have surrendered your mind, you cannot run from your karma, or your hands. In that final moment, you will know it is your choice only which ties and binds the knot of debt. Nothing else does the deed."

Looking back to the pouch, Hui added in anger, "Can such arrogance be tolerated! What are we to do?"

Only then did Bao Ling understand why he had been sent. Like Sying Hao, Shi-Hui Ke had seen through the foibles of man's raging ambitions. Like Sying Hao, he made his decision to remove himself from their arena. He chose to care for his own. Now, Sying Hao beckoned for his friend to return to the path of practical righteousness. To stand active once again as brothers and draw down Yama's sinister energies before the West and far South were brought to ruin.

Hui looked to Bao Ling, "Could you feel the weight of sorrow and loss as you traveled with this?"

"Most certainly, sir."

"How could you bear it?" asked Hui.

"I gave my word to Sying Hao. But for that, the cries from within would have driven me mad."

"Yes, that's it. The cries. So you do understand?"

Bao Ling only nodded.

Almost as an afterthought, Abbot Hui spoke, "I hope Sying Hao didn't have to kill a regiment to get this."

Taken aback by the scope of the comment, Bao Ling answered, "No sir. Perhaps you'll know what I mean when I say this. The treasure was passing through the southern highlands, protected by a company of trusted armsmen. Sying Hao walked into their camp one night. He joined them in eating and drinking and studied their revelry. Later he explored, found, then walked out with their treasure. A treasure which I later learned was to be funding and subsidy for further penetration into the west."

Hui grinned broadly, slapping his leg, almost spilling the contents from the pouch, "Of course I know what you mean. Sying Hao, that old fox! Right under their very noses, and I wager they never knew he was there!"

Zhi Mei studied their exchange intently, taking it all in with her poet's eye. When Abbot Hui first took the pouch and turned to Bao Ling, she thought for a moment tears had welled in his eyes, the fire's dance clear in their reflection. She knew what needed to be reconciled for any of this to make sense.

She asked, "Abbot Hui, if I may trouble you? What connects you to Sying Hao?"

Though surprised at the directness, Bao Ling welcomed the question.

Hui turned to Zhi Mei, answering, "Before happening upon you this afternoon, I had been sharing my story with Bao Ling as we descended the mountain. It closed just before I told of how I first met my comrade Sying Hao. Truthfully, little sister, the tale will make no sense if you don't hear it from the beginning. Begging Bao Ling's indulgence, I will re-visit what I shared with him earlier, and pick up with what followed. But perhaps we should first respect the late hour and save the tale's end for a better time.

"Bao Ling, just so you know, Sying Hao delivered this to me for two reasons. First, he wishes me to return it to whoever remains of its rightful owners. Second, he wishes for me to prevent its ever being taken again. You see Bao Ling, Sying Hao has a great gift for not using words to carry long winded messages."

Bao Ling looked intently at the fire and nodded his head. Staring into the flames, he pondered fate's loom and the guiding hand now warping threads intricately through their lives. All lay there before him, but beyond his ability to comprehend how any of it defined what must be. He felt unseen tides beginning their turn. He wondered how it all connected to the stream of time, and their own respective roles, whatever they might be. Did Zhuge Liang control the course of that stream too?

Hui humored the dimming fire, demurring to the late hour. Bao Ling and Zhi Mei needed to rest and recover their strength. But Bao Ling wouldn't budge, until extracting Hui's promise to tell all in due time.

And in due time, that's what he did.

A Dragon Could Do Worse

Next morning, Bao Ling woke to the clashing of weapons in the courtyard below. Acting on instinct, he quickly secured a perch on the rooftop where he strung his bow and maneuvered to survey the surround.

Occasional glimpses of dueling swordsmen crept into view, as well as armed combatants in full battle regalia. Some pushed forward, some retreated. Uncertain of just what he was seeing, Bao Ling steadied his hand and waited carefully. His thoughts still clung to his broken sleep. Could this be an attack? Who was who? How to distinguish? He watched for signs.

He knew this from long experience: generally, it's wise to exercise restraint. An act in haste is often regretted. In spite of what we think we see, beneath all images playing before us, there sit empty mirrors of truth, informing those able to connect to what they reveal. Bao Ling saw the eyes of Zhi Mei flash furtively from an opening to his near left. She glanced his way, looking for a sign. After considering a bit, Bao Ling laughed to himself. He tapped his left hand palm down, twice over the right, signaling the all-is-well to Zhi Mei. Though his judgment had clouded briefly, Bao Ling remembered what he knew with certainty only yesterday. The fortress stood impregnable. They were the only ones at the bridge. This could not be a surprise attack. That left only one likelihood.

Before them stood Shi-Hui Ke's warrior monks, now at morning play.

Then, in the corner below, he glimpsed Hui. Broom once again in hand sweeping about the busy legs of the combatants, occasionally even swatting one in the rump. Or doing a lightning disarm of another's blade. Sensing eyes upon him, he turned about to spy Bao Ling concealed on the roof. He laughed, then called, "Little Brother, what are you doing up there. The roof birds are our friends. Why frighten them when they threaten no one?"

The combatants broke cadence momentarily, savoring the jest on Bao Ling. Found out by their master! Their demeanor turned serious enough when Bao Ling leapt one level to the next, descending to the courtyard in three graceful bounds, landing like a cat alongside Abbot Hui. The rest quietly returned to their practice. Perhaps now with a bit more resolve, newly motivated by admiration for the stranger.

"Early mornings we practice, late mornings we meditate. Meals are taken at mid-day in accordance with tradition, and then we tend the temple and surrounds, particularly the plants, medicinals, and edibles. As you likely understand, we live in a harsh environment. Still, it nurtures nearly ample to our needs, almost to the point of self sufficiency.

"You'll find the grounds surrounding our sanctuary contain an enclave of mountain people. One-time refugees from the east, they have populated this refuge since the days of Liu Bei. Zhuge Liang came upon them and realized they would perish if measures weren't taken. So now this is their home. They are full partners in all our endeavors. They handle our trade, and it is their eyes and ears which constantly study for changes in the Shu Roads, and in the villages and towns below. You should take opportunity to mingle with them while you're here. They are very curious about you. I'm sure you know, your reputation has preceded you."

"Reputation?"

Abbot Hui pulled out yet another parchment offering reward for the elusive Dragon of the Midlands. He passed it to Bao Ling. "Yes. Whispers along the roads told of a new hero emerging in the province of Jing. When suddenly he disappeared. Stories of his exploits have buoyed hopes for the mountain people, assuring they were not alone in their plight. The tales gave promise that elsewhere, others worked equally to the same ends: a restoration of life itself, and a return to the simple values of brotherhood, equality, and freedom from the interference of others."

"These damn things are becoming a nuisance! No doubt they'll be the death of me. And what do I even have to do with all of this?" asked Bao Ling in earnest.

"Bao Ling, is it you who now chooses to deceive? We both know you are the Dragon of the Midlands. Mind you young man, without full trust between us, what do we have?"

Bao Ling read Hui's plea and answered, "Then fate dictates we move forward, partnered till death?"

Hui nodded, "It appears something or someone has already made that decision for us."

Bao Ling chuckled, "Partners with a mountain ghost and a one-armed monk who shoots thoughts. A dragon could do worse I suppose."

For once, they both laughed. Bao Ling did not know this, but Hui saw much of himself in the young man and was very concerned over the younger's fate. He also worried what would befall the beautiful young companion. Being associated with Bao Ling marked her. She would certainly be the first target of any assassins looking to shock and isolate their intended prey.

Thinking of Zhi Mei, Hui suggested, "Bao Ling, the monks will be escorting Zhi Mei to mingle with the villagers. You know, they're all very interested in both of you. It would be good if you explore a bit on your own. Go to the village. Take this opportunity to discover them. Learn to trust their congeniality and allow their curiosity to bring you together in friendship."

Bao Ling thought this wise, and quickly agreed. Besides, years had passed since he felt the comfort of simple community without having to worry about protecting his back.

As the men parted, Hui's thoughts were troubled. He was no fool. For him, there could be no doubt. Mercenaries, just like those who once abused him, were surely already dispatched. What wouldn't they bring upon the pair to secure their fortunes? Already, new legends unfold, telling of a young dragon riding on tales of heroic, seemingly impossible deeds. Behind him, a telltale trail of corpses among those who would have abused. Hui thought back to his own youth, and the tragic lessons of a lifetime. All pushing to an end which now seemed even more uncertain and rolled further back from his view. He hoped that for Bao Ling, it would be different. Unable to resist the thought, he wished, at the very least, Bao Ling would go out with all his appendages still in place.

Abbot Shi-Hui Ke

Part 7

You Are What You Do

The Village

Hui chuckled to himself admonishing his foolishness. Conceding what he could not control, he turned again to his monks in practice. One can only influence so many things. Beyond that, one is left with self-reliance and the friends he or she chooses. He called out to his students. "All of you remember. You are not dancing. Strive to be real. Actualize who you are when you move. Flow like water, dance lightly like the wind." He laughed, then pushed resolutely through their midst, his subtle moves off balancing all in his path; mere flicks of his torso or wrist catapulted their weapons off into space.

As Bao Ling made his way, he heard echoes from Hui's playful banter wafting toward the hills. For Bao Ling this assured his connections with Hui and the mountain people were as real as the rock beneath. He wondered if, way back when, Zhuge Liang had felt the same.

Before long, his trek toward the village drew the attention of workers in the fields. As he had seen their footprints delicately imprinted in the meadows, it didn't surprise when he sighted yaks in the distance. They grazed calmly, their human tenders nearby playing wind flutes to the sun. He knew even here, there were many layers to life. Slice away ambition, greed and the reaching for power. Magic and beauty soon drop in on their own. No different than anything else sprouting from the void.

He sensed footsteps approaching from the rear and turned to see a young mountain man nearing. Perhaps still a boy, but clearly a flock tender, and armed accordingly with bow, arrows, and blades.

For appearance's sake, Bao Ling had adopted a hunter's trappings, and stood practically attired, much like the boy. Perhaps nostalgia, maybe thoughts of home, he also preserved the time-honored woodsman's markings, delineating heritage, family and village of origin.

"You're him, aren't you?" the boy-man asked.

"I suppose I am, whatever that might mean."

"You're the dragon man! Everyone is talking about you. How the warlords have hunted you, how you've disappeared and re-appeared, taken from the rich, given to the needy, cared for the weak, and heaven help whoever moves against you. And … and your skill with a bow. We've heard of your lightning shots and your uncanny accuracy. Some mountain people even compare you favorably to our finest, Hung Lian Liu[18], but perhaps that might be stretching it too far, no offense intended good sir."

---

[18] Red Faced Liu. Fabled archer memorialized in Shu lore.

"Well, I'm just a man who hunts and tries to survive. It's true, my people suffered beneath the onslaughts of opposing armies, sometimes from the north, sometimes the south, perhaps the east, then again from the west. Wrong place, wrong time. I did a few things to survive, and helped others too, when I could. Nothing to boast about. I'm just trying to find my way back before what's left fades completely."

The young man nodded somberly, "And my hopes are with you good sir. If I may be of service, be sure to ask."

Bao Ling, looked him over, "Well, when I need a capable companion to cover my back, it's good knowing I'll be safe here in the highlands."

The courtesies continued their play, "I am Bao Ling of Ling village, a place once blessed with life and contentment, now a dust strewn void."

"And I am Kuan-Yin Ting, once rootless and adrift, until taken in by the Shu-Ting tribe, whose herds I now tend."

Bao Ling thought the young man might prove of use, then asked, "Can I trouble you for a favor? I am naturally awkward with strangers, and not acquainted with ceremony and customs in these parts. Might you accompany me to the village and assure I am properly introduced to the elders?"

"Most certainly sir."

The boy arranged for companions to tend the herd in his absence. The two joined company and descended to the lowland bowl where the main village lay centered. On approach, both heard the lilting currents of Zhi Mei's voice, already commemorating the prior day's events.

The attitude in the village was light, almost festive. The day clean and bright. No signs of outsiders or troops anywhere, nor any expected. This was their sanctuary. Here, among all places, they were safe. Bao Ling turned to Kuan-Yin Ting, "Is it always like this little brother?"

"Like what sir?"

Answer enough thought Bao Ling who, noticing something in the distance appearing like archers engaging, inquired, "What's that."

"Oh, we Ting people constantly work our martial skills. We know our destiny depends on it."

"Destiny?"

"Of course. Our eventual return to our traditional home in the eastern mountains, once they are freed of occupation."

Bao Ling acknowledged with a simple, "Good!"

As they approached village center, they heard light traces of Zhi Mei's tale of the prior day's adventure. Spun within her silken song, the account captivated and pulled nearly everyone from what they had been doing. Finding the village elders was too easy. The old ones fluttered around the nightingale no differently than the children at her feet.

The tiger closed upon me from behind
Savage intent lit from its eyes

Upon their hues of golden yellow
Floated two black pearls set deep within
Open portals to thoughts remote
Leading where, who can begin?
Here, today, its regal domain once secure
Majesty rendered by our footsteps impure

Discreetly it came, a stalking phantom drawing ever near
At first I glanced, then scrambled. Then nothing there
Till I felt the lightest touch of probing stare
Ah here you are! Quick, a reach for my darts
Four shots, eyes so delicate a part
Even for you great beast, a false start

We meet more closely. Now it circles, something new
Facial lines, patterned by timeless hand
"You encroach strange one, what shall I do?"
A studied gaze, ground quaking roar, flashes of ivory
Mules bellow their panic, such a sound
First terror, then warning, a plea to gather round

Moments seem to spin as days
All now mute. And stilled, but for the beast and I
A fog enfolds my thoughts. Look now! Crouched, it readies ...
A sudden kill will bring quick end
Clear warning to all, "My home, I defend!"
I will not fall so easily my friend

Pole and jian raised high
Arms spread, my screams touching sky

I see you waver great one, perhaps to wonder why
One frail such as this will not so swiftly die
Now just we two, white crane and nemesis circle about
I see your ready shudder, in protest I raise loud my shout

A shaft drops between. My companion returns
Beware beast, he gives no uncertain terms
A moment's pause, then four more
Now a blunted hit, leave quickly lest mercy shut its door
The weighted silence churns. You've had fair warning
Do not tempt fate's hot iron to burn
It grows late. Best now you should remit, and learn

A final look from stalled cat my way, recalls harsh memory
Who knows what one has no means to see?
But for this, from this feline's purge I will not be free
A tremble, a shiver, then a feeble shake
My fear, against me, now comes awake
A bolt of lightning descends to mark my end

I never saw the shot
But heard the punishing hit
Bones split, the great beast raced off to its shadowy pit
There on the bridge, my friend, and an old bent one
An armless archer, shooting empty bow unstrung
What magic? From nothing, such weighted thought far flung
The beast, all purpose shaken, now with restraint outdone

Bao Ling arrived just as the narration finished. He
reached for Zhi Mei's hand and lifted it high, proudly
proclaiming to the crowd, "But the real hero was the fearless

maiden, who single handedly held the beast at bay, saved
the mules, and without flinching, ruled the day."

Zhi Mei beamed for an instant, then shyly retreated from
the crowd's acclamation. The people here understood
courage. Particularly standing one's ground when the
situation seemed hopeless. Perhaps it was that thought
which then tilted their focus to the man now in their midst.

Whispers buzzed on the periphery. "It's him, the
dragon-man." Zhi Mei caught the shifting of attention,
amidst waves of curiosity. She looked to the one beside Bao
Ling and signaled with a nod for him to say something.
Young Kuan-Yin knew it fell to him to open the moment.

"I have been asked by my new friend Bao Ling, once of
Ling village, Jing Province, to make proper introduction to
our elders, and our people." Turning to politely address the
elders, he continued, "We have all heard stories of a great
warrior from the eastern plains. One like us, who had
fought and resisted valiantly against all oppressors, taking
only the side of the weak and the abused. His deeds and
exploits have found their way into our songs. There they stir
our determination to someday show the same fortitude and
excellence in returning our own land to tranquility and
prosperity. Honorable elders, family and friends, I am
humbled by the privilege and honor to ask your warm
welcome to Bao Ling, little brother to Sying Hao of Southern
Mountain, and sworn comrade to our own Shi-Hui Ke."

Taken by the introduction, Bao Ling's thoughts raced to
the question of how his young friend had learned so much
of him. He had arrived only yesterday. Then it made sense.

In this community, word traveled fast. The Shu-Ting moved with common purpose and single mind. Anything worth knowing was shared. It meant survival. He stood momentarily motionless, nodded his gratitude to Kuan-Yin, then faced toward the elders, preparing to bow respectfully. But to his surprise, they had already fallen prostrate. Within moments, the entire village mirrored their example, grounded in respect, and whispering "Dragon" amongst themselves, as though reciting a mantra of hope.

Who We Are Today

A stunned Bao Ling stood solemnly, baffled by it all. No less taken was Zhi Mei. Shi-Hui Ke must have known but had said nothing. Composure finally regained, Bao Ling lifted his hands signaling all to stand. He tried several times to speak before his voice returned. "Friends, honorable elders, please. I am not deserving. Here, come gather close about where I can look into your eyes and speak the truth of who I am. Then you will know I am a dragon without wings."

He hoped to speak candidly and articulate the truth. But the more he tore away at his legend, the more admiringly they nodded their heads and glowed appreciatively. In his huntsman's garb, his tall, evenly proportioned torso projected strength and solidity. Since taking up with Sying Hao his body had thinned and defined. Or as Sying Hao would say, the muscles relaxed away and the ligaments assumed their proper stature. His dark hair was tied back and his face lined by exposure. A well-trimmed outcrop of chin hair heightened the sharpness of his features. He looked like a primed steed about to sprint. They saw much of themselves, or what they thought to be themselves, in him.

Finally, hoping to quell any further misunderstanding, he confessed to the crowd. "I can see that you think of me as special. As one possessing principles and high motives, a protector of the old ways. With honest heart among friends, I will speak the truth. That is not who I am. Bao Ling of Ling village is a lost child, forever homesick. Driven by invaders to live like a jackal, he survived at first on scraps and garbage. Lurking in shadows, he struck out with murderous intent against any perceived threats. These traits do not deserve anyone's admiration. I consider them part of a great failure, a failure of the empire, of the contestants for power, of rulers, magistrates, generals, elders, community, and mostly of myself.

"Conflict has plagued our great land for generations. Surely even the heavens tire of this bloodbath. Man's unbridled ambitions push hard, now threatening to counter the natural course of Tao. Some predict the end is near. Others even hope it comes sooner, resigned to their sorrowful fate. I think otherwise. I trust action. I do what I do, and side with the impatience of the oppressed.

"I reject the tormentors' game which has cast us adrift these years. It's because I've spurned their game, they've proclaimed me their enemy. Fine. Yes, I've had to push against the tide, and yes, I have killed unhesitatingly those who meant to do me harm. But I am haunted by those memories, not bettered. The thought they were once as innocent children never fails to declare the grossness of my deeds. I do not forgive myself. Like many, they too were led astray by pipers pledging hope and better life on their mounds of clever lies. Until encountering Sying Hao and the poet maiden (he looked warmly to Zhi Mei), I walked alone and lived like an animal. Each morning I woke, expecting my end before sundown. Friends, take my word on this. Choose your destiny well and pick your heroes wisely. If you knew what I was, and the things I did just to prolong my meager existence, you would turn from me this instant.

Silence rippled through the crowd. Zhi Mei understood now, as not before, the weight of regret and conscience forever gnawing at Bao Ling. How had her poet's eye missed this? Her heart crumbled at the thought of his pain, and what had been the loneliness of his path. Bao Ling heard her sobs from where he stood at the front, vaulting to him over the fresh murmurs of the gathering. He felt warmed by her compassion and knowing she understood.

The oldest of the tribe stepped slowly forward, aided by companion elders. An ancient man, appearing almost to be immortal, he stood directly before Bao Ling, and carefully studied his eyes. He noted they were yellow over greenish brown in tint. A good portent. Not unlike those in the images of the famed Colonel Sun, a hero even more revered by the mountain tribes than the one standing before him. Though a small child at the time, the elder was old enough to remember seeing Sun. For a brief moment, his thoughts turned to the day the prince of warriors came to his own remote village.

By then Sun had already achieved his awakening; though it yet remained for his compassion to reconcile the violence of his past. The village received him as a demi-god. Sun would have none of that, allowing only that if merit were his true measure, they had every reason to drive him out. How similar the two. Unlike Sun, this Bao Ling was clearly no demi-god. He could have passed for any mountain tribesman in the first shining of his middle years.

The old man further remembered Sying Hao, Sun's youthful companion, a fine warrior in his own right and a masterful archer. Who could forget the time when he, and Li Fung trekked east into the already occupied hills? Against daunting odds, they recovered the presumed dead corpse of mountain brother Shi-Hui Ke, now the revered and seemingly ageless Abbot. It is said over two hundred enemy lost their lives in vain efforts to capture the two, hoping to avenge the disappearance of the ten sent beforehand to take Shi-Hui Ke. Yes, all rare heroes indeed. Just like this young man before him. How does one measure this special essence? From what deep well does it spring?

He waved his hands about, urging the crowd again to silence, then faced Bao Ling, "Young man, we have your advantage this morning. You see, nearly five generations have passed since I roamed these hills freely as a youngster. I remember when life itself provided all. You know what I mean. Food, safety, comfort, companionship, knowledge, love, understanding, skills, heritage and the promise of tomorrow.

"Then, one day they came, along with their silly agendas and designs on everything. You'd think we had no minds or purpose of our own. Always promising to us more than we had or had any right to have, and insisting it was moral and just to put our selfish wants first; to go for 'it' whatever the 'it' was. In little more than the passing of a season, what had sustained us now seemed lacking.

"Their fancy clothes, baubles, lust for power, and their bothersome habit of exploiting lessers to service their needs. It offended us at first. Our youth however, wanting for the lessons of life to see through the emptiness in this, were taken in. Even some leaders among us fell prey to the allure of their ways. They rejected the culture and customs of the hills and took up with what they predicted would be 'the future.' Not surprisingly, our youth became their underlings, and our maidens their concubines, or worse. Once torn from our ways, young spirits were soon broken. They had nothing to anchor themselves to. Some tried, but never seemed able to return, or to heal. Some disappeared, some took their own lives, some possibly met the likes of you, and perhaps got their just deserves.

"It pains me to say these things, but they must be told. You're not to blame. There's more than enough failure to go around. As you already made testament, they deserved better had they the courage to stand for something true. A number of them secured their success and prestige, at least for a fleeting moment. They brought the pests into and through our lands. Thus usurping the very hills and passages which had been our identity and nurtured us through the ages. We too took to living like animals and doing what we had to do to survive. We blood swore to preserve the carcass of who we once were, if only to rekindle what remained for when the tide turned. That's who we are today.

"No different than you!"

Deshi Ku

Meeting Deshi Ku

"As I've already said Bao Ling, we have your advantage this morning. Stories and songs do not deceive us. We know exactly who you are, and what you have done. We too have lived and walked your path, cast from our roots and ruthlessly hunted. All of us have watched helplessly as friends and relations suffered unspeakable abuse. Often having no recourse but to beg a merciful death.

"As to judging your deeds, and your character, we have seen ruthless killers, and we have witnessed heroes. Think of yourself as you will. You must trust we can distinguish the two."

The kind words overwhelmed Bao Ling. He had always acted from necessity but it did not ease his conscience, or his sense of personal culpability. He wished those he killed had never chosen to cross his path. They had their reasons. He had his. Those who died at his hands also had families, parents, children, wives, companions. None of whom would have any interest in Bao Ling's justifications or rationalizations for taking the lives of their loved ones.

Still, the Chieftain's words closed a fault in Bao Ling's spirit, assuring, "We know what you did. In a troubled time where there are no clean choices, you acted with righteousness and chose not to compromise what you valued most." The warrior stood, quaking with grief, but also with relief, over the weight now lifted from his karma. He felt a touch to his right. Zhi Mei had worked her way alongside, where she studied his opened soul, revealed by the moment. In time, she would come to sing this man's praises for all.

Kuan-Yin then intervened, to ensure Bao Ling received proper and formal introduction to village leader Deshi Ku. He was the ancient one who had just spoken. After paying respects to the chieftain, they next made proper acquaintance with the others.

Among them were Li Kong the bridge maker (and destroyer), Dishi Jou, the man who watched the waters (and studied the underground), and of course Li Fung, martial master and legend in his own right. They say his family had lines running back to Liu Bei. It was his broad and proven skills in tactics and weaponry which assured their ableness to continue against daunting odds. He had also mentored Shi-Hui Ke from early childhood, and it showed in their constant reliance upon one another.

Bao Ling later learned elder Deshi Ku had filled many roles over his countless years. From warrior chieftain, to trusted counselor, and supposedly occasional sidekick to the legends Sun and then Sying Hao. Most importantly, as he matured through life and gleaned the essential experiences, he mastered the healing arts. His insights into the workings of the body benefited all. So too did his studies of the mind and spirit.

Had Bao Ling not encountered Deshi Ku on this particular day, and had his choices and actions not been cast into this new light of perspective, he would not have survived the season. His mind and spirit would have become lost to false emptiness and despair: the hero's unceasing burden.

Might all of this also have been the doing of Sying Hao?

Deshi Ku then invited Bao Ling and Zhi Mei to accompany the group as the elders congregated to dine and to counsel amongst themselves. Deshi declared, "We'll gather on the hill overlooking the village, and watch the hawks coast on the winds." He begged the people return to their affairs. In due time they would all have ample opportunity to make better personal acquaintance with their guests. For now, Bao Ling and the poet Zhi Mei were his responsibility and charge.

Bao Ling petitioned that Kuan-Yin Ting, his "squire" might also accompany, not yet knowing the mountain people deemed the right to sit with elders as one to be earned by trial and long proven merit. Kuan-Yin was noticeably discomfited by the suggestion. He politely begged off, explaining he had herds to tend to and the guests were now in better hands. Deshi Ku, quick to assess and reconcile, ordered: "Kuan-Yin, the herds will be fine. Who better than you to ensure the continued comfort and wellbeing of our new friends? Join as we dine, then plan on how best to accommodate the needs of our honored guests during the limited time we have to share their gracious company."

Kuan-Yin Ting wasn't saying "no" to that!

Requiring no prompting, no sooner had they gathered when Zhi Mei performed her poetry and songs. Her improvisations memorialized Crystal Springs and the other retreats as citadels of hope, assuring a return of the people to their ways of harmony and joyful life experience. One could almost believe it true on hearing it from her. When done, she pressed the elders for more insight into the characters of Colonel Sun and his companion Sying Hao. Several times she raised the question to Deshi Ku, "Was Sying Hao a ghost, or mountain spirit? As Sun's one time companion, would he not have passed from this life long ago?" Her own words embarrassed her when she instantly realized Deshi Ku had earlier been said to have shared their company. What to make of it all? She thought all the while of Bao Ling's report. Sying Hao appeared mature, but not elderly. And physically quite robust, likely evidencing his years trekking the wilds and surrounds of Southern Mountain and the distant southland.

Deshi Ku always spoke truth, and in answering Zhi Mei, encouraged, "What is important young niece is that he lives. As do I. He served as squire and attendant to Colonel Sun, and also even as apprentice to Zhuge Liang before the wizard's untimely passing. Most of these things occurred well before my own time. Yet even I would not deem it fair to call him an old man. At least not as old and worn as the one you see before you. As a youth, orphaned by war he walked our path. Alone and abandoned he had much in common with my people. But something shone within him which caught the compassion and admiration of two sages. One a warrior prince, the other a paragon of human potential. To think of him as a ghost would do him great disservice. He has forged a long trail. Of one thing I am certain. He, for one, will see it to its end. Someday perhaps you'll meet him. Be sure to ask him these things yourself. If you and I meet again, let me know how he answers." Then laughing, he made sure to add, "And if he shares any good secrets, bring them too."

Bao Ling caught the reference to Sying Hao as once apprentice to Zhuge Liang. And also the reference to Zhuge's untimely passing. Just as he started to ask Deshi Ku about the connection between Sying Hao and Zhuge Liang, an unexpected visitor interrupted their discourse.

Kong Kong Upsets the Elders

They called him Kong Kong. His name, by its sound, almost a moniker attesting to his great strength and boundless energy. When others spoke his name, it sounded like the bottom of a closed fist pounding a door. They couldn't help it. Almost everyone had their own involvement with him. For that reason, he achieved notoriety both good and bad as student and disciple of Master Li Fung.

Among the Shu people, threads of traditional skills connected everyone in the community. Prominent among them were martial skills, and the healing arts. Herders weren't just herders, nor were growers simply growers. From the youngest age, those in the tribe knew the survival of their ways depended on broad diversification of talents. Each member of the community must be able to fill the shoes of others should they be lost. In short, they could all fight just fine. They also knew how to heal and treat their general wounds and illnesses, to hunt and forage, and to resist adversity. That said, even by their own high measure, and what they knew from hard experience, this young man stood apart. Kong Kong, above all others, was a natural born hellion in the raw. Who could control him? Who could rein him in? Who could save him from himself? Not one among them had the answer.

From childhood, he excelled at the martial arts. The venerable Master Li Fung would long ago have recognized him as his finest student, but for one thing. No one, including the Master, could govern the lad. Not even with Li's own powerful example of discipline. Like water rolling off a rock.

The youngster could be a stallion at times, and definitely had his own mind. One which did not always sit well with his teacher's. Was there even a conscience in there? Master Li had seen it before; a great talent rising under his tutelage, but not under his influence. He could only set proper example, and hope for the best. Sometimes, but not always, it was that very example which made the difference. One thing he would not do. He would not crush the boy's spirit. *Always,* he thought, *teach by giving the best possible example. Never suffocate what you hope to nurture.*

There had been others, and they had turned. They tended to be the ones most easily beguiled by the allures of the outsiders. Promises of wealth, fame, and adulation drew them like metal filings to a lodestone — eventually aligning them with the designs of oppressors. Only when realizing the ultimate price did they come undone.

You see, warrior talent can be harvested from just about anywhere. Truly, despite what some would have you believe, it's not so rare a commodity. It just takes the ability to bend conscience a bit. And the enemy sought to harvest those like Kong Kong for one reason above all. They knew how to unravel the many riddles within the Shu Roads.

It went like this. First they were cultivated, tempted, enticed or captured. Then brought in. Their talents, whatever they might be, would be lauded, showcased and praised. Assurances would be given. Promises made. They would not have to engage their own people or savage their own lands. They would be deployed elsewhere, against remote threats, and their achievements well rewarded. There, they would have opportunity to realize their full potential, perfecting the complete array of warrior skills while administering to and quieting uncivilized barbarians.

Eventually, the dark hour would come. They would return to the eastern court as field hardened and battle tested knights, now of unquestioned loyalty. Only then would they be assigned the traitorous task.

Guide an army from east to west. Lead them through the Shu!

In that moment, their ripened folly lay fully exposed. Their allegiance had been sorely played. Sadly, it was this awareness which usually proved their undoing. Having grown accustomed to their new world, they had forsaken the simplicity and purity of mountain life. Fortunately, at least until now, not one had freely chosen to fully violate the sanctuary.

What became of them? Unable to return home, some became bandits, some warlords. Some had to be eliminated by their own once-benefactors if only to set convincing examples for the others. More than a few simply lost their minds and fell to naught. Naught. The ultimate price of folly. Li Fung feared for Kong Kong more than he had for any other. This one had the potential to do or be anything; but Li Fung had not been able to harness his spirit. Late evenings, when alone, he often lit incense and prayed the boy not be lost.

All knew. Broadly talented as he was, Kong Kong had one particular skill in which he took greatest pride. As an archer, he had no equal in the community, or for all anyone knew, anywhere in the great land.

Still encumbered with the ardor of his aspirations, Kong Kong had long yearned to test his skills against a worthwhile opponent. Now, a stroke of particularly good fortune. In their midst had come a "legend." As noteworthy an opponent as he had ever hoped to encounter. Too auspicious a sign to ignore, Kong Kong determined he would ride the advantage of kind fate and finally carve his own mark. He knew full well, the time to strike was when the opportunity presented.

A stroke of luck like this could not be ignored. It might never come again. He had already seen Bao Ling, and taken his measure. Nothing about him intimidated, at least not at first glance. Studying him, all Kong Kong could make of the man was how much he looked like a typical hunter. But then he noticed something more. His arrows, and his bow. Though simple and unadorned, they exhibited a level of subtlety and craftsmanship Kong Kong had seen only from the skilled hands of Master Li. Such tools and attention to detail made it clear: Bao Ling was not one who would cater to chance. The implements spoke much of the artist and left no doubt as to his yet unrevealed skills.

Today, he would throw the challenge! Defeat Bao Ling, and he would become the new legend.

That's how youth thinks you know. And among the Shu, that's what parents and elders like Li Fung hoped to guard against, and never to encourage. Li Fung knew it made for much trouble.

Like others, Kong Kong had heard the stories and songs celebrating the "Dragon of the Midlands." Uncertain as to their basis in fact, he still regarded the tales with envy and awe, wishing one day he too might rise in courage and endurance to match the deeds attributed to this legend from afar.

He entered the forum in his usual brassy way. Seeing Bao Ling, he thought, *Never in my wildest imaginings did I expect the myth to show up in our midst. Think of it. Here, in the middle of nowhere.* With no innate sense his conduct might prove offensive, he charged doggedly forward to the very seat of Deshi Ku, demanding, "Venerable sir, I must have a word with you."

Troubled by this breech of protocol, Kuan-Yin, sitting to the right of Zhi Mei, bent forward and looked at Bao Ling to her left, "I apologize in advance for my comrade's impertinence."

Bao Ling shrugged his shoulders, turning his hands upward, questioning, "What?"

But in an instant, he knew. Kong Kong's stare fixated on Bao Ling. There could be no mistake. He was the subject of their exchange. The solicitation of Deshi Ku pertained only to Bao Ling. The hairs bristled on the back of his neck. "Even here," he whispered to himself, "no respite."

Zhi Mei turned to him on hearing this. He looked to her, but his look told her nothing.

Deshi Ku leaned to Master Li Fung and the two traded words. Li Fung firmly shook his head with an admonishing "No!" directed straight at Kong Kong. His reddened face left no doubt to the degree of his feeling on the matter.

Dejected, Kong Kong backed away, bowing respectfully, then snuck a quick final glimpse toward Bao Ling as he turned about.

Just as he started to move out, Bao Ling called, "Little Brother, come close. Since you're here, please allow this humble guest the honor of your acquaintance." He turned to Kuan-Yin trusting he would do the formalities for both.

Once acquainted, Bao Ling asked the now surprisingly reticent Kong Kong what had prompted his visit. Might there perhaps be an emergency? Is assistance required? Someone in distress? How might he help?

Kong Kong

Part 8

An Unexpected Challenge

The Weight of Vanity

The elders recognized the tone of the banter, and
patiently let it play its course. With his careful words, Bao
Ling was stewing the young man in his own juices. Kong
Kong now stood alone on the "hot spot." Here, he held the
center of everyone's attention — which to his chagrin
included the inquisitive scrutiny of the fair poet maiden. He
froze where he stood. A most uncomfortable sensation of
warmth reddened his face.

But like all ordained to be warriors, he somehow found a
way to regain his center. He determined this hot spot suited
him just fine. If that be the best which fate delivered, he
would take it. He turned to Bao Ling. Now with renewed
confident eye, he entreated, "With no disrespect sir. Archery
has been my life's passion, and I too have some history of
exploits and accomplishments. Mere shadows to yours of
course, but certainly worthy of life's measure and attention.
In my impertinence, I asked blessing of the elders to
challenge you to an archery competition. Forgive me sir, I
see now I had fallen prey to my own vanity."

Bao Ling could only smile. While not a vain man
himself, Bao Ling knew well its consequences. None other

than Guan Yu, invincible in battle, the equal of thousands, allowed his vanity and sense of self to be sugared by a young officer of the Wu. The officer, whom we will not honor by naming, had devised a plan using an appeal to Guan's own carefully cultivated self-image. With that, he created vulnerabilities within him never found on any battlefield.

Already an older man, Guan had witnessed the decimation of his once invincible forces, as well as the desertion of many others. When alone, he began to wonder, *Am I becoming extinct?* But even then, he remained unassailable and free, no mortal man his match. Until that fateful day when the young enemy officer entered his camp under flag of passage.

He pleaded friendship and admiration for the legendary warrior. "Sir! I request only the honor of a polite meeting. Since childhood, I have long admired your deeds and accomplishments."

Guan, ever generous, saw no purpose served in beheading the audacious young admirer. Instead, they spent the evening together drinking and re-visiting many of Guan's legendary exploits and encounters. In due time, plied by the never emptying cup, the old warrior wearied, and bid his young new friend good night. By morning, the war god was no more. The young officer returned to his lines confirming his success. None among his own believed him. Until arrogantly, he proved it by brazenly mounting the great general's head on a stake.

"What would be the nature of your challenge? Certainly not a fight to the death, I hope?" inquired Bao Ling.

Kong Kong looked to Bao Ling, puzzled. The question surprised him, and in no small degree, had him confounded. Why would the honored guest even think such? Then it dawned on Kong Kong that with Bao Ling it had always been to the death. Challenge meant only one thing. To survive.

Bao Ling stared at him dispassionately, waiting in silence.

"No sir, a friendly match, to showcase our skills. No one gets harmed, we compete as friends."

Bao Ling stared at the young man. After prolonging his silence, he replied, "Please forgive me. I am confused. Are we friends? Do I know you? Have we met before this day?

"Perhaps it is a difference in our customs. Where I hail from, challenges seldom flow from true friendship. You see Kong Kong, with every competition something is gained and something is lost. Out there, where fate has no patience with errors or lack of precision, victory is life. Anything less is death, or perhaps something worse.

"Even in a match among supposed friends, which is what you propose, fate wiggles its finger, stirring what had been before into something completely new. Things change because of it. For some, the possibilities become their motivation, for others, their bane. For example, if we have a contest, and I win; well, then I become the hero who tried to enhance his reputation by showing up a boy. I see nothing in the victory for me. No one likes heroes who do that. Now I'm not claiming to be a hero mind you, but people will think what they will, both good and bad.

"You on the other hand, will gain boasting rights about having taken on, and perhaps having bested Bao Ling. Should you upstage me, some of what they say of me will then pass to you. I will return humbled to the shadows, moving about in anonymity. Trying all the harder to survive as more just like you will want whatever pieces remain. Then almost surely, they will turn their gaze to you. I can't imagine you would find that extra weight comfortable to bear. My point is such things can never be taken lightly, particularly during these times. Too much depends on us being exactly who we are, and having the mind to manifest our true natures with courage, dignity and conviction, letting nuance and image fall away.

"Just think for a moment how far I am from my home. I am here but a day, and already I am challenged. What would the outsiders think of you should they hear you had defeated the Dragon of the Midlands? Perhaps they would coax or cajole you into joining them? Perhaps they would forget me, and then place my bounty on your head? I'd be fine with that. Do you wish these things for yourself?"

Kong Kong's face glowed red with embarrassment. He had no answer for any of this. Now He started to wish he had never entered the assembly. If only he could find the words to extricate himself from this predicament.

Allowing ample time for the silence to register among those present, Bao Ling looked to Deshi Ku. "A friendly shoot off. I trust Master Li Fung will consent to lend his skilled eye as judge?"

Deshi looked to Bao Ling, "If it is our guest's wish, and meets with Master Li's approval."

Li Fung responded by standing and issuing the classical martial bow of respect toward Bao Ling, inner left hand over knuckles of right, projected at chest level. He figured maybe someone else could give the boy the lesson he needed. This kind stranger might be the last opportunity to save the lad.

Bao Ling knew from his gesture and respect the judging would be impartial. In reciprocating the gesture, he accepted.

He turned to Kong Kong and said, "It's not for me to quash the opportunity you so eagerly pursue. Be careful though my friend. Sometimes, when you get what you wish for you may find its weight difficult to bear."

The others present, laughed at the thought, knowing all too well how getting what you want most is more often what you justly deserve. You might not like where you end up.

It was late next day before a suitable site could be cleared of animals and cordoned to where contestants had clear range. Villagers, herders, shop owners, traders, even the monks and nuns began to cluster about, all looking for where they could catch best view of the anticipated spectacle.

As it turned out, word spread quickly of the event. Others also eager to show their skills were soon lined up as contestants. It grew bigger by the moment.

Not completely surprising to the elders, Bao Ling welcomed all who wished to partake. He took careful opportunity to have Kuan-Yin introduce him to each and share a bit of each's history to cement their identities to his memory. By the time shooting commenced, there was a field of twelve village contestants, and just as many warrior monks, twenty-four in all. Even Kuan-Yin (at the urging of his new friend) had joined in.

Initial targets were set at 50 paces and the group agreed each would have five shots, after which the ten highest scores would advance to round two.

Initially, it hardly resembled a competition. Everyone seemed to be having too much fun. Except for Kong Kong, who remained deadly serious. In his own mind, any carelessness or lapse would lead to indelible loss of face. He could not have that.

Master Li Fung, not one to let drama slip his grip, saved Kong Kong and Bao Ling for last among those in the first round.

The Dragon Is a Fox

When it came time for Kong Kong to shoot not a single whisper could be heard from the crowd. The first shot rifled straight to target's center. Bao Ling offered his congratulations, saying "Not since I first met Sying Hao in a remote lowland field have I seen such a clean shot. I can see my work today should not be taken lightly." Kong Kong knew he still had four shots to confirm and advance his effort. He wanted a quick and convincing start.

The next four shafts sailed nearly as perfectly, netting the highest score possible. Only one other contestant had hit center, and that with three of five.

Bao Ling dropped to one knee down. He placed the shafts alongside resting their tails aside his planted foot. He took a deep relaxed breath, cleared his mind, then fired the five shafts in rapid succession. Three of the shafts hit center, the other two flew off into space. The crowd moaned disappointment. Li Fung saw what the others did not. Bao Ling had just fired five shafts in little more time than it took for the relaxed eye to blink and open, or for one to draw a full breath. The complexity of the feat, and the ease with which it had been executed brought back memories of Shi-Hui Ke in his prime.

Kuan-Yin, armed with only the expectations of youth, stared in disbelief, "Two missed the target. How can that be?"

Bao Ling answered, seemingly unconcerned, "I get better when the stakes get higher." Zhi Mei simply marveled at the speed and grace of the arrows flocking with common mind to a determined end. For an instant, she thought them all airborne simultaneously, a wondrous achievement. Then decided her eyes were playing tricks. Or were they? The fact two missed detracted nothing from the grace and symmetry of what she had seen.

Abbot Hui laughed and poked his elbow into the side of Deshi Ku (almost knocking him from his feet), "He's no dragon Uncle Ku, he's a fox!"

Kong Kong had no idea what to make of it.

You see. As an archer, Bao Ling tended to relax on the draw. Accolades, kudos, and recognition meant little more to him than did the temptations of power, wealth and influence. He was simply satisfied. He made do with what surrounded him and drew joy from the changes unfolding. Kong Kong and perhaps the others had something at stake, or something to prove. Not so for Bao Ling. With him, nothing could be proven — except that he gave each moment his best.

Bao Ling's torrent of five arrows, shot in an instant, provided a measure. Abbot Hui (being a comparable spirit), along with Li Fung, and perhaps even Zhi Mei saw and understood what others failed to discern. As the shafts covered their trajectory, both Hui and Bao Ling studied their oscillations and drift, taking full measure of the influence of wind, moisture, and temperature on the accuracy of their flight. Eyes serving minds like theirs could freeze the flight of hummingbirds while their scrutiny revealed secrets invisible to others but were nonetheless there to be gleaned.

From the original round, the ten with highest scores advanced to the board-splitting competition. Kuan-Yin stood jubilant as he and another tied at tenth, and the elders, with no objection from Bao Ling, agreed both should advance to next round.

Board splitting required great focus and concentration. The boards were curved bamboo slats, planted firmly in the ground, standing approximately chest height. One forearm's length down from the top, a yellow dot could barely be seen from across the 75 paces to where the archers stood. A direct hit on the dot nearly guaranteed the board would split. Missing by even a hair's breadth meant uncertainty, missing by more would deflect the arrow off into space.

Again, each had five shots, the top five would advance based upon total number of boards split.

At 75 paces, even a slight unanticipated nudge from the breeze would send the sailing shaft astray. For that reason, this exercise required patience, awareness, and stillness, traits not common — particularly among young or less experienced archers.

The first, a villager, the second, a monk. Neither could muster a split, though both made consistent contact with the boards.

As the rounds unfolded, and the degree of difficulty became evident, Kuan-Yin grew anxious. Seeing his turn nearing, he huddled beside Bao Ling to ask, "Master, I am a fish out of water; how does one reconcile all that can change in the moment. Please sir, how to untangle this puzzle?"

Bao Ling looked to his young friend, now seemingly become his protege. He thought how, had they met in Ling Village, he would have enjoyed the brotherly company as he, the elder, guided the youth through the early onslaught of life's lessons. Much like his grandfather had done with him.

His answer held no surprises. "See only the yellow. Still your breath. Release your shot only when you determine you can delay it for not a single moment longer."

"Got it! See only the yellow!" the herder replied. Then he stopped cold. "What in Yama's hell does that mean?"

Bao Ling looked hard at Kuan-Yin, then delivered a lightning slap with his right hand to the young man's forehead. Once the shock settled, he repeated slow and succinctly "See only the yellow!"

Though knocked back several steps and stunned senseless, from deep within the clearing haze of Kuan-Yin's thoughts, the words reverberated, "See only the yellow!"

He certainly saw yellow then. Responding to this high pat on the horse's head, Kuan-Yin could only mumble, "Oh."

No time to lose. Kong Kong stood at the ready, Kuan-Yin positioned to follow, then Bao Ling waited patiently to shoot last.

Kong Kong froze in space, watching the breeze dance over the tips of lingering blue bells. He waited intently for all to still. Just when time rolled to a complete stop, he let his arrow fly, then nonchalantly turned away. As he reached for his next shaft, the anticipated crackling of splitting board rippled over the crowd, which had already seen the spectacular disintegration of the target.

"See", Bao Ling said to Kuan-Yin, "like that!"

The elders overheard and thought perhaps Bao Ling might be taking the event too lightly. Kong Kong was not one to be toyed with. For them, this was serious stuff. All villagers knew of Kong Kong's remarkable deftness with the bow, and many expected the day to be his, no disrespect to Bao Ling intended. His own courage and skills were already proven by past deeds, but even so, for them Kong Kong's talent stood singular. They had all seen what he could do.

Though still early in the game, some muttering could already be overheard. In person, the "legend" seemed quite ordinary, and up until that moment, a fair but unremarkable archer. A few even went so far as to call the stories about a dragon in the midlands mere tripe.

Knowing better, Zhi Mei recoiled on hearing this. She had seen the man in action! They hadn't. Her face flushed red in embarrassment for her friend, and then her angry eyes flashed toward those leveling their cheap shots. She would make this right, and already a song began shaping within as she carefully studied what was to unfold next. Boldly, she pointed to a cluster of doubters, then called out, "They Spoke of My Friend."

They spoke of My friend
When they reckoned his deeds mere tripe
"The Dragon of the Midlands" such hype
He's my friend, and has my trust
I know only him, the man you see
And the echoes of his past deeds
Foot treads in timeless dust

There, they speak of a dragon
He's my friend
I have seen him as the Dragon
and as my friend
I know only him, and what I've seen
and the words we've shared

Others proclaim his past deeds
Tales which defy all imagination
stretching one's belief to its far end
Can anyone do what they tell of him
Such feats. Impossible you say

Hushed whispers, your lips declare your thoughts

But I have seen him as the Dragon
and as my friend
I know only him, and what I've seen
And his deeds, I dare not say
Believe what you may
Cross him, you will surely regret the day

See Only the Yellow

Kong Kong's subsequent three shots also struck true, only one more needed for an unprecedented perfect score. His final shot flew sure as its kin. Impact to the board appeared clean, but the board emerged unscathed as the arrow glanced away from its well-trimmed path.

Disappointment lined Kong Kong's brow. He wanted that shot! Those close by could hear his whispered curses to the wicked strands of devious fate which stole his arrow's mark.

Kuan-Yin stood next and readied. The crowd could hear him talking to himself. Endlessly repeating the mantra, "See only the yellow. Still your breath. Release your shot only when you determine you can delay not a moment longer." The other competitors found it curious, a sure sign of his inexperience.

Some in the crowd deemed it funny and laughed. Clearly the young man was overwhelmed. Some still rooted for his success, while their hopes faded.

At first, nothing. He stared at the targets, which seemed a moon's distance away. In fact, what he knew to be 75 paces might just as well have been the other side of the valley. He could scarcely see the board, and the yellow mark seemed to have vanished. Was it ever there in the first place? He signaled for Li Fung. "Sir, could you check the board's marking to ensure it had been applied?"

"No need to check Kuan-Yin, I placed the yellow mark on this board myself, same as with the others."

Kuan-Yin retorted, "But I can't see it. Are you certain?"

"Yes, I am looking directly at it as I stand here beside you. Same as all the others. No difference whatsoever."

Having embarrassed himself, Kuan-Yin could only turn to Bao Ling for support, but found his nod confirmed Master Li's affirmation. Then, abruptly, Bao Ling walked to where Kuan-Yin stood at the ready and whispered something into his ear.

Kuan-Yin, eyes tearing in desperation, nodded his apprehension, and readied his first shot. He held his draw, quieting his breath, matching his stillness to the dance of the air. Then he pulled yellow from where he thought it stood in the distance. Until the bright circle seemed nearly touching the tip of his arrow. He adjusted for elevation, then listened, holding any release until a carpet of silence blanketed nature's breath, assuring stillness for the flight of his shaft.

He wasn't certain as to the timing, or how he chose it. The moment of release declared itself, and he simply got his hand out of the way.

The arrow flew like a bird. Sprung free with a mind of its own, looking for safe perch. Kuan-Yin stared almost in disbelief as the path held true, and the shaft seemed drawn to the standing board. Pulled toward its home through the yellow ahead.

The loud crack of contact, then the arrow flitted away, revealing the board still solid in its wake.

It felt as though everyone groaned in disappointment. Even the earth beneath his feet seemed to echo the sentiment.

Both Bao Ling and Abbot Hui appreciated the trajectory's clean path. A true shot indeed, even though an overly resilient target frustrated the youth's deserving effort.

Hui whispered to Bao Ling, "The fault lay in the herder's tools, and not in the talent. A better crafted bow might have made the difference."

Bao Ling nodded agreement, "We'll have to spend time with him on this."

Bao Ling looked again to Kuan-Yin hoping to encourage, but the young man assured in return. Confidently, he tapped his forefinger to forehead miming toward Bao Ling, "See only the yellow!" No doubt the high pat on horse's head had driven the point home.

The second shot also ricocheted. The crowd again registered its disappointment. If even possible, their collective groan resonated more viscerally than before. They saw no difference between his shots and those of Kong Kong. Whispers of "bad luck" and "mountain spirits having their fun" bandied about. Even though a miss, Kuan-Yin actually felt assured and confident with the effort. By his reckoning, he had let fly two nearly perfect shots. But for unkind luck's fleeting interference, he might be standing there with two confirmed hits.

Bao Ling saw the youth's confidence had steadied. Their eyes locked. Bao Ling lifted his right hand, forefinger hooked for Kuan-Yin to see, then twisted his wrist inward in a gesture Kuan-Yin immediately read as a signal to hold steady. Success will come from doing the same as before but striving harder. Bao Ling knew ill fate rarely tricked three times in succession.

Hui ambled alongside Bao Ling. "What did you whisper earlier to the lad, to quell his anxiety?"

Bao Ling answered, "I told him if he and I didn't get our shit together, we might both be forgotten men by day's end."

Hui nodded and smiled. "Nice touch."

"We'll see. He has three shots left. The next will set the tone for his confidence and what follows."

"Yes," agreed Abbot Hui.

By then, all the villagers stood alongside the range. Some hoped, some prayed. All wished for the young man's success. Kuan-Yin had lost his parents and family in one of the many past incursions from the east. But not before his loving parents named him for the goddess of compassion and carefully oriented his pliable young spirit to that end. Despite his heartrending loss, he held true to his parent's wishes and fine example. He served all with love and empathy even though he be without household and lived often in the wild. Many in the village considered themselves to be his proxy family. It was said the guiding hand moved all of their hearts to steer the young saint whole and steady into his future. Within the community, he was nephew, brother, or cousin to all who knew him. That included even Kong Kong, though he for one, seemed to want little to do with Kuan-Yin.

As the crowd's attention focused, incense sticks were passed. Their fragrant aroma spilled over onto the field of play, until Kong Kong finally asked Judge Li Fung to discourage the distraction from interfering with the focus of the event. Seized by the moment, hastily erected food stalls interrupted their service as community chefs and servers also collected with others to the sideline. All knew what happened next required their contribution to the positive energy directed to the youth.

Elder Li Fung told Kong Kong he had already shot his limit this round and had no status to make request at this time. In courtesy, he looked to see if Kuan-Yin had any like concern, but the young archer already stood, lining his shot, and mapping the ever-fluctuating atmosphere. In fact, he liked it. The delicate energy of drifting smoke and mingling odors of incense, threading against background aromas of fares simmering on charcoal coals allied with his study of the wind and its lapping currents of air.

This proved to be a new experience for the young man, perhaps precipitated by or in reaction to the stress of the moment. As he sighted over the field to his intended target, trails of vapor and aromas on the light afternoon breeze signaled corrections to be made in his aim and trajectory. Almost defying solution … so much compounding together. It unfolded as an added dilemma, demanding his remedy. He felt the drift of atmosphere, first one way, then the other. Now up, then down, some elements canceling out, others teaming together. Where within this sensory maze might he find the requisite correction necessary for reliable aim at the instant of release?

He sighted his bow and steadied for some time, the complexity of calculation forcing beads of sweat to gather on his brow. Nearby, Kong Kong began shifting impatiently, first to one leg, then the other. "Should I correct for that too?" thought Kuan-Yin. He could hear Kong Kong's impatient exhale.

Finally, not feeling adequately rooted for the shot, he lowered his bow. If only to breathe and relax, and to run new assessment on the prevailing influences. From the corner of his eye, he caught Abbot Shi-Hui Ke staring intently. Abbot Hui, as had Bao Ling, lifted his right hand, and hooked his index finger, driving home the point of Bao Ling's already signaled order to "command the moment."

Abbot Hui of course, having mastered the thought arrow, may have thought to intervene. We can only speculate what he might be capable of. No one, except perhaps Bao Ling and Li Fung would have known. We'd like to think he freed the moment to Kuan-Yin's destiny. Such opportunities can never be planned, nor should they be subjected to interference or meddling. Their integrity lay inherent, and need always be respected. Especially by supposed monks. Would that kings, emperors, and warlords knew to do the same!

The Archer's Mantra

As Kuan-Yin took more time, the atmosphere of anticipation only heightened in the crowd, now starved for more. Returning to basics, he relaxed. Starting first at the ground below, then at the dantian, he concentrated on allowing his own internal winds to catch the governor's circle. At least that's what others had told him should happen. Beads of sweat trailed down his face. In the silence, he noticed the errant smoke standing frozen in his field of view. Birds crossing moved straight to the flap of their wing, and the wildflowers rested. He quickly lifted the bow and drew to shoot, holding only for the moment to reveal itself. He steadied his breath, remembering to keep weight to the underside and relax completely. It was then a veil lifted, and his fingers eased their grip on the bowstring. The shaft raced forward like a hawk in pursuit of quarry, head keened, wings tucked, feet lifted and pulled in.

This time Kuan-Yin held his release pose. He wanted no after ripple of movement on his part to cloud the arrow's purpose. For a moment, it looked to all as though the arrow grew outward from his bow, extending in straight line until ramming square center on the yellow mark. With the explosion of the board, the vaporous trail disappeared.

The crowd erupted in admiration. All agreed when even Kong Kong approached the young man, declaring, "A magnificent shot Kuan-Yin. Savor the moment!"

Kong Kong, like some others perhaps, thought luck had smiled on the young man. The tone of his voice said as much. More experienced eyes, like those of Master Li Fung, knew that if luck had intervened it acted maliciously to steal success on the first two shots. But not this time. The shot showed a maturity and level of skill and patience not expected in so young an archer. The elder watched intently. He knew what followed next would mark the measure of the man, and perhaps forever change Kuan-Yin's role and responsibility in the safeguarding of his people and their ways.

The fourth shot fell prey to an errant dragonfly, whose own fate deemed its end married to the tip of Kuan-Yin's otherwise well taken effort. A small deflection indeed, but enough for what amounted to little more than an excruciating near miss.

Kuan-Yin murmured to himself, "How often does that happen? What can possibly go wrong next?"

Only five competitors would make it to the final round, Kong Kong had four hits, two others had two, Kuan-Yin and two others had one. Without question, he expected Bao Ling to qualify for the next round, so only one slot remained for him to make the cut. Kuan-Yin's advance would only be assured if his final shot proved true.

Earlier that afternoon, in a brief moment together, he asked Bao Ling how he managed to function in times of gut-wrenching stress. It troubled him greatly. The uncertainty of how or if he would hold up. Specifically, he questioned what raced through Bao Ling's mind when surrounded by enemies in what seemed to be situations without hope.

Bao Ling answered, "There can only be one thought which, if nurtured carefully, will free me to act in all planes, without fear or trepidation."

"And what thought is that?" the young man asked.

"That I am already dead."

"That you are already dead?" the young man repeated incredulously.

"Yes. Perverse as it seems, it is your only freedom. You see, the minds of attackers are riddled with distractions and temptations. Fears polluted with hopes of reward, opportunities for alliances, gaming nefarious manipulations, posturing, then reticence, trickery, deceit and even treachery. It's a marvel they can even stand under all that weight.

"This broiling stew virtually ensures they are thinking of themselves, their survival, and then their ambitions — but not enough of me, their destiny, or the consequences of their miscalculations. Their minds slog awkwardly through a muddled field of play. But for their ruthlessness and unbridled cruelty, they'd hardly be able to plow a path through all the nonsense. Only if you fear for yourself, or the consequences to you, will you find trouble playing to the best of your ability. Better simply to give it up, to decide you are already dead. Use that stick to stir the mud, and you'll be amazed at what surfaces from within.

"Having nothing to lose, one moves freely and with full purpose. Since you asked, I will tell you truthfully Kuan-Yin. At times it seems they are so stuck in their imaginings that I might simply just walk away, or even step right through their midst. In fact, I have seen others do just that."

The words baffled Kuan-Yin. Being a youth meant his thinking followed common threads. Completely predictable and rolling about in two dimensions. In so many words, Bao Ling encouraged him to push through the gates of perception — and to unmask the freedom of reality beyond. Was there indeed such a place?

Seeing the befuddlement, and tying the lesson to the moment, Bao Ling went on. "Take today's competition as an example. Never let greed for victory get in the way of actualizing your true self. Ride the passing moments to find your best within. Let your actions prove your merit. Before you start, assume you have already lost, then go forward freely."

Kuan-Yin thought, "Savor the moment," now recalling Kong Kong's taunt, and the hint of condescension in his tone.

There is no moment. Nothing to savor. There has only ever been the one shot. The arrow's tongue, not Kong Kong's, will ultimately tell my story.

Forgoing thoughts of victory, or continuing to the next stage in the competition, or even of wondering about Bao Ling's earlier imperfections, Kuan-Yin went deep within himself. Sinking down, he extended his Chi, touching the distant board with his gaze, sighting the yellow mark and bringing it to where he stood. The late afternoon wind had increased, the air had cooled and changed directions, now running its way downward toward the valleys. This would be no easy effort. Everything before him seemed to dance and come alive once more. Movement became evident everywhere under the first influences of cool evening's soon to be weighted atmosphere.

His thoughts passed on to Bao Ling, knowing he had yet to take his shots. His friend would have to contend with these unpredictable breezes and the rapidly diminishing light. Only then did he completely understand. Shooting last, under these conditions, Bao Ling had little chance of clearing the round.

One would think this only made Kuan-Yin more determined. Admittedly, it's hard to speculate on the machinations of a mind now nearing empty.

"It doesn't matter about Bao Ling, or about me," he whispered. "I have already lost. See only the yellow. Still my breath. Release the shot only when I cannot delay a moment longer. But never too soon."

The archer's mantra.

For a moment, things shifted a bit. Kuan-Yin no longer focused outward, looking to isolate every subtlety of the environment. He also gave no further thoughts to dragonflies fouling his intent.

Now, it was only he, or should we say, his inner awareness. For that was all he felt. His arms and legs had disappeared moments before. The bow, string, and arrow, all merely a vane riding the course of his will, manifested through his intent. Then, in a flash of certainty, he angled the sight line of his bow relative to his center, three thumb's widths to the right, correcting for the breeze, then raised the tip's arc high over forehead, deciding in the instant to loft the arrow to its destination, rather than spiking it, and tempting fate to intervene yet again. It made no sense, but he knew it to be right.

He held for his moment, and when he could delay no more, released.

On release, Bao Ling turned to Hui and smiled.

The shaft glided sleepily over its long exaggerated arc. Some wondered, would it even have enough momentum to split the target? For the crowd of admirers, time stopped. All eyes riveted on the descending missile.

The cracking board opened a deluge of cheers and spontaneous outpouring of emotion over the young man's accomplishing what earlier that same day, had been deemed far beyond his capabilities.

Kuan-Yin walked over to Kong Kong, "Abbot Shi-Hui Ke once told me. First time, perhaps luck. Second time, luck stands aside and admires."

Kong Kong could do nothing, no longer seeing his young friend as a hapless competitor, nor someone out of his element.

Kuan-Yin had made his point, settled in fact by his accomplishment. Kong Kong took the young man's arm and raised it high, signaling the moment belonged to Kuan-Yin, and deservedly so. His eyes grew moist as he did this. Something new.

Competition Advances

Five contestants remained for the next round. Despite Kuan-Yin's concerns, Bao Ling somehow managed three splitting hits as darkness descended and the early evening winds wreaked havoc. The crowd studied closely as Bao Ling released his shafts angling upwind, perfectly calculating the downwind spiral for each arrow's winding path to somehow return it to the yellow mark on the boards. With each of the five hits, the crowd stood silent. Three were perfect. Two ricocheted without shattering board. These were no ordinary shots. They had never seen anything like it. Arrows which corrected in three dimensions, as if by magic, reconciling and pushing through whatever sought to twist their path. All knew the real contest began here. Even Kong Kong gave credit to the achievement, but not before declaring he could have done better. Hearing this, Bao Ling smiled and shrugged his shoulders, making sure Kong Kong saw his words were only words.

Li Fung carefully weighed several challenges of appropriate measure for the next round. He wished to up the ante for the five remaining contestants. Something different, more complex, a challenge which would test skills to their very limit. Four of the contestants clustered eagerly, impatient to be tested and distinguished. Bao Ling stood alone, apart from the group, as still as a post.

In the end, Li Fung opted for the running target.

The target doesn't actually run. It consists of a block of wood, about the size of a man's head, suspended and riding across the width of the range, at 100 paces. As I'm sure you can see, even hitting a stationary object at that distance requires superb skill. To facilitate this challenge, elder Li Kong, the bridge maker and engineer had his helpers sling and tighten cables across the field. In the time it took for all to pause and refresh with tea, the apparatus materialized into readiness.

Master Li Fung explained the target would run across the field of view from left to right, or right to left, depending on his random draw. Each contestant would have seven shots to stick four targets. If any contestant failed to stick four targets, he would be eliminated. If no one managed the feat, the contest would end without a winner. If more than one succeeded, most hits would determine the champion. In the event of a draw, there would be a final round, so long as light permitted. All agreed, and as mountain people tend to do, each contestant turned to the other to offer words of encouragement. Not expecting to see this, a smile briefly lightened Bao Ling's now focused demeanor.

Elder Li Kong demonstrated the mechanism, calling for one of the targets to glide across the field of view. Except for Bao Ling, now seemingly busy coaching his protege, the complexity of the arrangement drew everyone's scrutiny. Bao Ling had his own way of seeing things. While being hunted in the midlands, his skills of awareness became keen. Not so much from conscious effort on his part. More like a familiar within which had awakened to stand vigilant, wary and ever ready. An ally which in time had become indistinguishable from the host.

Though not always seeming to be paying attention, Bao Ling knew as much about his periphery as he did about what stared him in the face. Sying Hao appreciated the value of this remarkable gift. Under his demanding tutelage Bao Ling had perfected the art of doing multiple things at the same time. That played especially well for him on this day, and in this moment.

Though busy placating Kuan-Yin's trepidation, Bao Ling took careful note of all which unfolded — particularly the demonstration now underway.

He saw how Li Kong's apparatus allowed for the target to come into quick momentary view, and then to accelerate rapidly on the down glide. The time for calculations, and judgments of conditions reduced to near nil. There was too much happening, and too fast. Even the most experienced archer would barely have time to draw, sight, judge, lead and release. A remarkable challenge, and a credit to Li Fung's ingenuity. Thankfully, as he knew to be typical once darkness settled in, the wind had started to ease.

Still, until full darkness, late day conditions would threaten moment to moment with intermittent gusts and shifts. This factor further compounded the issue of time lost waiting to see from which side the target first emerged.

The first two contestants could hit none. Their shafts whizzed errantly off into space. Both walked away shaking their heads and muttering, "It's Impossible!" Deferring to their earlier performances, Li Fung seeded Kong Kong and Bao Ling for last. He reminded, "Boys, a little suspense only enhances the pleasure of the experience. Let's give the folks a good show." Bao Ling assented to Kong Kong's suggestion Bao Ling shoot final, as that would befit the distinguished guest. Forget courtesy. Kong Kong of course had taken measure of the rapidly diminishing ambient light and left nothing to chance. Going first might ultimately determine who won.

Kuan-Yin, who was next, volunteered to switch places with Bao Ling. He, as did many in the crowd, recognized Kong Kong's manipulation. Bao Ling declined. He already knew to keep his focus on the big picture, and to let the games of others less experienced have their play. The problem to be solved lay in the timing and not in the lighting. Besides, like Li Fung, he wanted the folks to have a good show.

Most importantly, going first might help calm the young Kuan-Yin.

As Kuan-Yin prepared to shoot, Bao Ling caught his attention and signaled by separating his palms in the air. The palms framed his lips as they whispered, "lead your shot." Then he spread them even further, as if to say *lead more than you think is necessary.*

Kuan-Yin's stomach turned topside down. He couldn't find his root. Though he stood there intently, inside he had become someone toppling from a cliff, wriggling about in space, going who knows where, and not knowing how to land cleanly.

He held his bow and shaft at the ready and waited. All stood silent. A sound, from the right. The slide of target over cable, already midway, a rushed shot, far behind as the target cleared the field to the left.

Now he knew why the others had whispered, "Impossible!"

In later years, Kuan-Yin would recall fondly and with awe what he gleaned from that afternoon. "A day with Bao Ling stands equal to a year with any other master." In retrospect, he resisted the temptation to conclude the entire day had been for his benefit. Could anyone be so skilled at manipulation? He entered as a young herder, and left with new confidence in his skills, and in his person. Somehow, under the guiding hand of Bao Ling, his universe had shifted. Things impossible became routine, things unsee-able became clear. And once changed, he never reverted to his old ways. The guiding hand of Bao Ling left its permanent brand on the young herder's spirit.

The second target also emerged from the right. This time Kuan-Yin's thoughts raced like lightning, he ran his measures, calculated and released, sending a shaft which closed like a hawk on the target, sticking nearly center, just as it crossed mid-range.

As with Bao Ling, the crowd silenced, perhaps so as not to disturb the young man's heightened awareness. Or simply shocked someone managed to hit the target at all.

A practical young herder, Kuan-Yin, trusting conscious analysis, weighed the probabilities, and anticipated the third target would emerge from the left. The error cost him needed time, as the target again dropped from the right. Before he could compensate and shoot, it had crossed center and left the field.

Judge Li Fung ruled a shot would be counted against Kuan-Yin for opportunity missed. One out of three.

Fourth pass imminent, Kuan-Yin's mind began playing tricks. Li Fung studied him closely, as he knew this would happen. It had been in the conception of the challenge's design. Kuan-Yin struggled to keep open view of the whole field, but couldn't let go of the odds now favoring entry from the left.

Another opportunity lost.

Fifth pass, now fighting to clear his mind. He found his eyes darting left then right then left then right then left. It was as if he never even saw the target until it seemingly lingered from friction, midway, as if to taunt him.

One out of five.

He turned to Master Li and asked if he could stand back for a moment, before the final two targets passed. Li turned to Kong Kong and Bao Ling, who had no objections. Kong

Kong of course welcomed the delay. It promised to make lighting more difficult for Bao Ling.

It's not easy not to be distracted. Only now did Bao Ling's comment about "already being dead" begin to make complete sense. It seems we are attached to everything, all the time, and don't have the wherewithal to let it go. The young herder laughed to himself, "We're even attached to nothing. You can think you are not distracted, or you are freeing yourself from distraction, but even that is yet again distraction, and in effect, an impediment." He glanced to Bao Ling. Bao Ling knew well the look, and he turned away. Even that, a message, thought Kuan-Yin. Bao Ling himself had become yet another distraction for the young man, one that out of respect, simply turned away. With two shots remaining, now it fell to Kuan-Yin alone to steer away from distraction; and to recognize his old muddled and distracted self was "already dead."

He turned to the field and set. He no longer cared whether the target came from right to left. When the target emerged, he would see it, measure it, pace it, adjust, then shoot, trusting only his emptied self. Like a mirrored lake readily reflecting and becoming one with the reality of the moment. And he would be sure to do his best!

Number six was a hit. That alone quelled murmurs of "luck" for the first hit.

One shot remained: again, a hit. His final statement of competence to seal the lips of any who doubted his change. Three of seven.

Next up, Kong Kong.

Better if a Dragonfly Had Crossed

"The young man has considerable talent," whispered Chieftain Deshi Ku to Bao Ling. Alluding to Kong Kong, he continued, "Sometimes talent creates unrealistic expectations and leaves one frustrated with our ways. As you may know, our enemies consider this a fault to be exploited."

"No doubt true, Uncle. But the day lingers. Lessons may still be imparted and learned."

Deshi answered, "Yes, I will watch with great interest." He then made a martial bow of respect to Bao Ling and departed.

Kong Kong hit the first five targets with a precision surpassing any of his earlier shots. Clearly, he had his sights on only one thing at this point, besting Bao Ling. For the spectators, a breathtaking display.

Only when taking out the fifth did he consider he might have run his round too quickly. Had he missed one, and stalled, and perhaps missed another, Bao Ling would be left with barely enough light to see and shoot.

That very thought may have broken his focus. He missed the sixth attempt. Though visibly disappointed, he paused, then took more than usual time to scrutinize the conditions and strategize his next shot. In the crowd, some murmured displeasure over the inexplicable delay and the rapidly fading light. Perhaps splitting his attention on two disparate objectives diluted Kong Kong's focus. Though unmistakably intent on the seventh, he failed.

You see, even your will, should it weigh too heavily from its center, becomes distraction — yielding an arrow which cannot fly to its target.

Bao Ling, seeing the evening's shadows crawling across his field of view, quickly stepped forward and set.

No different than shooting locusts[19], he thought.

First target emerged, and the shaft had already released. Kuan-Yin did a double stare, *Had he shot before the target appeared?*

A direct hit, the target continued its run across the full field; arrow sticking anticlimactically from its center.

Kong Kong took note of the message, clearly meant for him.

---

[19] A reference to Bao Ling's past, and how he forged his skills. Full details can be found in our prior work, *Seed of Dragons*.

Next shot, Bao Ling waited, the target slid left to right, passing center, descending to the right, accelerating to where it would drop from sight, clearly too late for a confident shot. Only then did Bao Ling let his arrow fly. He directed the shaft to a spot far to the right. By then the target had passed from view, and just as it did so, only the loud thud told the crowd there might have been a hit. Bao Ling knew he had scored. No one else did, until Master Li Fung had the target recalled, and all could see the centered hit.

Kong Kong again registered what, between them alone, had been a very clear statement about who could do what.

Abbot Shi-Hui Ke turned to Zhi Mei, "Take note young poet, a dragon has just alighted in our midst."

"Do you really think he's that?" she asked.

"He is what he is. Study what he does. That is how you tell the dragon apart from the straw man."

The third and fourth shots registered hits at range's center, from the left, then from the right. There was a purpose to the pattern. In this final round Kong Kong witnessed Bao Ling execute with celestial precision what Kong Kong might only do if blessed with profound good fortune. He had no idea what test awaited should a tie necessitate a final shoot off. He didn't want it to go that far. He did know he feared losing face if he failed to succeed in the very competition he demanded of Bao Ling.

Fifth target slid right to left, exploding from the shadows and barely visible over the darkened field of view. With three shots left, and knowing the remaining targets would not be visible, Bao Ling shot early on first view, his second shaft launched before the first made contact, and the third shaft instantly thereafter.

No one can say for certain, but in later times, when the act played in their legends, the mountain folk spoke of three arrows borne to air just as the target emerged to cross their view. Kong Kong at first smiled, reckoning the shots ill-considered and impertinent. Driven by excess confidence, or desperation, with no chance of success.

"Show off!" he thought.

But Bao Ling's birds sailed home to their nests, just as he knew they would. The crowd erupted in astonishment as the impacts sounded across the field. One - two - three, just like that, just as quick as you might say it. To all appearances, he nonchalantly launched three shafts, appearing not to have a care or concern; with each striking home as the target raced its course. Just as the target passed midway, where ambient light left no room for doubt, all registered the miracle.

Kong Kong's spirit may have sunk to new lows, but to his credit he remained determined, at least for now. Dishonor or no dishonor, he prepared mentally for whatever came next. They had both scored five hits. Bao Ling had no shots left.

"I will show him my best!"

Satisfied he had seen enough, Li Fung begged the late hour, drawing attention to the darkness. In the conciliatory tone only a true elder could muster, he argued the diminishing light made continuation of the event imprudent. He smiled and added apologetically, "Besides, I've run out of challenges for the day." He looked to the remaining two contestants, asking "Would you be content declaring our friendly match to have ended in a draw."

Bao Ling would have gladly done so. By now he was minding Zhi Mei and the undue attention she was gleaning from the day's earlier, less successful competitors. He knew the way of things, and the drives of untamed youth. He turned quietly, deferring to Kong Kong, who answered first, "Sir, with all respect, the day's purpose stands unfulfilled if no clear outcome can be shown for the efforts."

"But I have no further test to set your skills apart, and night rests upon us." The elder looked to Bao Ling, "Your thoughts sir?"

"I have no agendas here Master Li, except to be polite (then staring at Kong Kong) and to properly honor my hosts." He removed the gold sovereign, which had been strung about his neck on a thread of leather cord running through its hollow center. He passed it to Li Fung saying, "Hang this from a cross beam at 150 paces. Set lanterns alongside. One shot each. Whoever can put his arrow through the center, wins the day."

Master Li looked to Kong Kong, who turned to Bao Ling and asked, "And what if we both miss?"

To which Bao Ling replied, "Are you planning to miss?"

Li Fung interjected, "If both miss, or if both succeed, I will declare the day ended, and the match a draw. At some point, all games must close. Life beckons we return to our responsibilities. Besides, I'm tired and hungry!"

Abbot Shi-Hui Ke's attention riveted on the two. With his experience, he knew the degree of difficulty of the contemplated shot. Why, it was impossible! No one could do it! Unless perhaps he were riding the wings of dragons.

Kong Kong shot first, at Bao Ling's suggestion.

As he lined the shot, he had second thoughts. Why couldn't he have simply accepted the draw? His insistence to move ahead only drew unneeded attention to his ambition, and his inexplicable need for recognition. Traits which even he disliked within himself. "Is it too late to change my mind? What would they think of me?" He might better have chosen to truly befriend Bao Ling, rather than try to cut a slice from his notoriety for his own self adornment.

Kuan-Yin studied the shot as Kong Kong surveyed carefully. The gold sovereign tempted from the distance, hanging lazily from its cord. There, it dangled from bridge maker Li Kong's hastily erected spirit gate. Master Li Kong, inspired by the moment, had instantly instructed his craftsmen to mount two pillars and an archway from whose truss the sovereign hung, flitting lazily, oscillating and spinning in the subtle breeze. To aid visibility, the elder set the sovereign high, nearly twice the height of an unstrung bow and sat two lanterns alongside the posts. The gold sparkled enticingly, a lure for any passing fish. Apart from its glow, Kuan-Yin could scarcely make out the coin, even when using his focus to enlarge it in his mental screen. It was hardly there, and at times indistinguishable from the hole in its center. *Like shooting a phantom, could anyone make this shot?*

Master Li Fung knew the outcome would depend on his trained eye to judge the authenticity of the hit. Even he questioned his ability to see with confidence, should the speeding arrow close on the coin's center.

To eliminate dispute, he called Abbot Hui to stand across from him. A second perspective, the trusted eye of Shi-Hui Ke might validate or offer credible second view on any decision rendered. In the event of split opinion, all agreed Deshi Ku would make final determination.

Kong Kong studied the target. Again, the empty feeling inside. He quivered in waxing vertigo. Were he alone, he might have puked. *This is the moment, all or nothing.* Even the thought of surpassing Bao Ling receded to the background as he wrapped his focus around the dangling shape and his bone tipped arrow, now smoothed to its narrowest measure. In silence, he attempted to reconcile the random movement of the target against the incessant spinning of his own internal compass and calculations.

Bao Ling approved the timing of the young man's release but knew there was a problem as soon as the arrow charged forward. Intimate awareness can never be harnessed by mere words, and no words or judgment crossed the brow of

Bao Ling as he saw the arrow close on the sovereign and knew without doubt it would miss the hole.

An audible click, the coin gyrated wildly in the air, and danced about on its cord. Could such an object mindfully mock an archer? Ask Kong Kong what he heard.

Li Fung declared the shot had struck the side of the coin. Then he confirmed for all, "It did not pass through center!" Abbot Hui affirmed.

Kuan-Yin whispered to himself, "How had they seen what my eyes missed?" Then he looked admiringly to Kong Kong, utterly amazed he had somehow managed to strike the coin. No one could fail to see the disappointment which registered on Kong Kong's face. Tears welled in his eyes as he stood alone. Kuan-Yin walked to stand with him, a friend when needed, then offered, "A remarkable effort brother Kong. You needn't be disappointed."

But Kong still had to deal with the sour taste of ambition unfulfilled. He turned to Kuan-Yin, at first angry, and about to lash out. Then for once, seeing the young man's generous spirit, he composed himself and spoke, "It would have been better little brother if a dragonfly had crossed its path and accounted for a missed shot, which otherwise would have stood true. Some might have said, "But for a stroke of poor luck, Kong Kong could have won." But truthfully little brother, the dragonfly was me, and the shot tempered only by my judgment, my character, and my hand ... missed."

Kuan-Yin held still, pondering the words, then answered, "What you just said brother Kong. That was the best hit of the day!"

Shooting Hole to Arrow

All eyes now turned to Bao Ling. He looked carefully through his assortment of arrows, while surveying the field and all movement.

Unlike Kong Kong, for whom focus was linear, Bao Ling's gaze saw in all planes, just as his ear heard in all directions. Some say people who see and hear like this are magicians or shamans. That they speak to the dead and can see the future. No, that is not true in the least. More precisely, it is not true that they speak to the dead and can see the future. Honestly, in that regard, they're just as much in the dark as you and me. But they do see what slips between the cracks of our perceptions. Our supposed reality. As the ancients taught us, it's in those overlooked spaces where most of the experience can be found.

Sort of like sliding down a snowy hill toward trees in one's path. Some people see only the trees, and everything they do reflects in some way the need to manage, and the concern if they're not careful, they'll hit them. Driven by fear, movement cramped by anxiety, they sometimes hit those very trees they're working so hard to avoid. Bao Ling had long since weaned himself from such tendencies.

Descending the same hill, he'd see the trees nested in a universe of space. He'd have no concern of running into even one.

While others saw obstacles or resistance, or felt anxiety or fear, he felt only like Bao Ling. Free. Not perfect of course; same as everyone, wrestling with purpose, struggling with righteousness and its price, working to survive, bemoaning failure, agonizing over mistakes or misjudgments, or past deeds. But fortunately, able to sometimes make reality shift ever so slightly to the better. Where, when it became most important, he might act decisively.

Distracted by some obstacles in his path? Never.

Overcome by challenges? We'll soon see.

Standing ready, he briefly considered the feasibility of intentionally missing the shot, allowing the young man his bragging rights at day's end. But what would be his truth then? He knew it would not quiet the tapeworm of ambition gnawing within the lad. The door had to be slammed shut, or the young man would be lost. Bao Ling had another strategy, one which he had begun to map far earlier in the day. This path pointed to a climax yet to unfold, and an opportunity for Kong Kong to find who in fact he really was, and perhaps return to his true path. But it posed risks.

Kuan-Yin's attention riveted on Bao Ling. He shared his mentor's stare toward the gold sovereign downfield. Bao Ling turned and smiled at the young man, touching two fingers to the younger's eyes then pointing the two fingers to the target in the distance. His lips moved as if to say, "See only the space within."

A light went on for Kuan-Yin. He realized he had been looking for the space within all this time but did not know where or how to find it. There it was! Bao Ling stood there like a Buddha, pointing the way, then finally turned toward him to affirm. Framed by the distant sovereign lay the endless space within, a realm of infinite possibility, giving shape to everything. All now opened before him. Following Bao Ling's true eye, he positioned behind, lining arrow with bow to target's empty center in the far distance. The void connected everything, bringing all together.

An impossible shot, he thought, then re-considered, *but not for him.*

Bao Ling let the arrow sail. Unlike that of Kong Kong, it was a soft shot, arching gracefully over the field, seeming to take forever. All could see the coin dancing on its cord. Spinning its far-off taunt at the incoming shaft. Kuan-Yin had just about forsaken hope and turned away when he noticed a final lethargic turn of the coin to its front, hole centering as if to greet the incoming missile.

Master Li Fung could not be sure what he saw. No sound emitted as the arrow seemed to pass through the center. But for its continuing rotation, the coin never moved or changed its course. The elder thought he had just witnessed a perfect shot, but it appeared too perfect. So perfect indeed, Master Li Fung did not have the confidence to say with conviction what he thought he saw. He demurred.

Kong Kong had already staked his ground, yelling out for all to hear, "A miss!"

Bao Ling walked to Kuan-Yin as all other eyes turned to Abbot Hui for his judgment.

"And what did you see little brother?" Bao Ling asked his friend.

Kuan-Yin knew what he saw. "I saw Bao Ling make an impossible shot, the arrow passed through the center of the coin, just as certainly as I am standing here before you."

Overhearing, Kong Kong scowled, trying albeit not too well to conceal his anger. His ultimate goal now so near at hand, he deemed his destiny set. They would all remember. He at least had struck the coin.

To Kuan-Yin, Bao Ling said (perhaps just loud enough to float to the ears of Kong Kong), "It's never enough to just shoot the arrow to the hole. A true archer knows to also shoot the hole to the arrow."

As Kuan-Yin and Kong Kong puzzled over this riddle, Abbot Hui declared the shot true, knowing from what he saw that Bao Ling had in his own way, mastered the thought arrow. It was all in the turn of the coin.

Kong Kong angrily disputed the judgment. Chieftain Deshi Ku asked Abbot Hui if he was certain. The Abbot simply stared in response. He was not one given to cavalier bias. Even Kong Kong took note and quieted. Deshi Ku conferred with Li Fung who affirmed his impression the shot had succeeded, but apologized for his aged eyes, declaring in this instance he could not confirm with certainty what he thought he saw. He asked his finding of "hit" to not be determining.

Since technically there was no dispute of the judges, Chieftain Ku had no say in the outcome. Still, leaving it as it were would only breed anger and resentment in the heart of the young warrior Kong Kong. Only one act could address this.

He walked directly to Kong Kong and asked, "Kong Kong, can you state with absolute conviction that you saw the shot miss?"

Kong Kong had the "Yes" set at the very tip of his tongue; and with all his striving heart, he tried to sail it out from that cliff. But that damned mountain righteousness bred into his person by generations of ancestors now reached forward, gripped the word, and buried it deep back into his gullet.

Pushing hard against what had earlier been the ascending tide of his young ambition, he answered, "No sir, I cannot say that with a true heart."

Like Li Fung, Kong Kong could not be certain of what he thought he saw. He turned to Bao Ling, half smiled, respectfully downed his head, and said, "My apologies sir. For my earlier outburst."

Bao Ling nodded his acceptance, setting the stage for Kong Kong's final passage into manhood.

Knowing the matter had not fully played through, Abbot Hui turned to the crowd, "We are most fortunate in what we have witnessed. Skills displayed today, convened on barely a moment's notice with no practice or preparation attest to our conviction and readiness to protect our ways, our land, and our people from continued exploitation and violation. But for one troubling point, we might all leave contented and assured. It concerns me that some will not credit the brilliance of the final shot by Bao Ling. Perhaps some will have second thoughts or opinions, in spite of my affirmation. Sadly, we are left with what we have and that will seal the day." Then he looked to Bao Ling, "Unless our honored guest can suggest a demonstration which will quiet all doubt."

Hui turned toward Bao Ling, and winked. The stage was his, the opera could run its course.

Bao Ling walked to where Zhi Mei stood, then spoke, "Zhi Mei, I need your help."

She agreed.

He went to Elder Li Fung and asked for one of the bamboo planks, matching the ones used in the second round of the competition.

He returned to Zhi Mei, handing her the plank, "You do know, I hope, that I would never hurt you?"

She nodded, "What will you have me do?"

"Go to the coin, stand beneath it, then take fifteen steps beyond, turn toward me, and wait. When I signal, hold the plank high and tightly over your head, in line with the coin. After that, it would be best if you tried not to move. Oh, and do try to smile. It adds to the effect."

After an admonishing stare, she moved faithfully to her post. By now, Kong Kong had begun to put two and two together.

The Finale

Bao Ling walked to one of the cooking pits and extracted some ash which he mixed with his saliva for all to see. He then traced the mixture along the feathers of his shaft.

By now, Kong Kong had reckoned Bao Ling's intention to shoot the arrow first through the center of the coin, and then have the same arrow split the plank, held high behind it by the maiden's trusting hands.

He could have none of this. It was insane. Why was it necessary? His eyes darted to Abbot Shi-Hui Ke for support, hoping he would intervene. Hui simply shook his head, "No!" Kong Kong trembled with anxiety as Bao Ling now turned to Master Li Fung.

"With your indulgence sir, I will prove my shot by replicating it in such a way all doubts will be dispelled."

"Explain," replied Master Li.

"The shaft will pass through the sovereign, leaving the mark of charcoal on the inner ring. Its flight will continue to split the board directly behind, held high by Poet Zhi Mei.

Once I make the shot, Kong Kong will have his chance to match it, if he so wishes the opportunity."

The elder assessed the difficulty and the near lunacy of the endeavor, "It is one thing Bao Ling, to put your own life at risk, but to risk an innocent to appease vanity," turning to Shi-Hui Ke, "Abbot Hui, please help me with this."

Hui turned slowly to Kong Kong, then spoke as though to the air between them, "An account not fully reconciled, leads only to mischief and misfortune."

Kong Kong felt the scathing heat of the words. It was his foolishness and vanity which pushed the day to this end. How to unravel this new maze without losing face, and without offending Bao Ling, or causing injury to the maiden? He turned to Bao Ling, "Brother, it is an impossible shot, and presents great risk to the honorable lady. There is no need for the day to end in tragedy and loss. Here, right now, I proclaim you the day's champion! You have bested me." He turned to the crowd and yelled for all ears, "I Kong Kong proclaim Bao Ling, Dragon of the Midlands, to be my better as an archer. His valiant efforts, and masterly final shot have held my inadequacies to the light for all to see. I accept this, and proclaim him winner of all. Come friends, let us agree to end the game, and celebrate his great victory!"

No one moved of course. Just as had Kong Kong's challenge from earlier in the day, what Bao Ling now proposed proved irresistible to their fancy, as he knew it would.

You can see how some things can never be put back in the jar, once they are let out.

Bao Ling walked to Kong Kong, and spoke only to him, "I hear what you say now, but I fear tomorrow you will not mean it. It proved to be an interesting day young friend. You cast your die without considering all possible consequences and outcomes. I would hope you learn to next time be more careful and considerate, being sure to take full measure of your self and the challenge, before demanding action.

Kong Kong mistakenly took that as Bao Ling's assent to conclude the competition, accepting Kong Kong's concession. His relief clear to all.

But then, Bao Ling turned toward the field, which had already disappeared into the black. Far in the distance, the white silken topshirt of the poet maiden shimmered in faint afterglows of fire framing her in darkness beyond. There she stood behind a suspended gold sovereign, which Kong Kong knew was there only on faith, as it could no longer be seen in the gripping darkness. Bao Ling nodded to Zhi Mei, she lifted the plank, He set his arrow, drew his bow … steadied … and …

"You'll kill her!" shouted Kong Kong, "No one can make this shot! Don't be a fool! This is pointless! I refuse to participate."

Bao Ling turned to Kong Kong. "Little brother, the shot must be made. That was clear from the beginning. You called for the contest. You chose to compete against my history. I accepted your challenge knowing only one thing might quell your desire to stand tall over my fall. Now, you will be my witness, one way or the other."

"Sir, I won't allow it!"

The crowd's discomfort became evident. Was this a threat? In the short span of one day, they had grown to love the poet maiden. Now, calls from their midst echoed Kong Kong as the drama played before them. But Kong Kong's behavior? That left them knotted. Some approved, some not. You see, in the village hierarchy, youthful Kong Kong lacked stature. He had acted far beyond his station in pursuing the contest, and now again, in making demands of the warrior Bao Ling. Abbot Hui, and the elders held their own counsel, and then their tongues.

Bao Ling turned again to Zhi Mei, then spoke nonchalantly, but in voice loud enough for all to hear, "I will agree to the archer Kong Kong, standing in place of the poet maiden Zhi Mei."

Abbot Hui again elbowed Deshi Ku, "The fox is loose!" This time, the elder turned and whacked the monk on the forehead with his palm. Perhaps in faux anger, perhaps not; both turned politely away from each other back to the field.

Kong Kong froze, he felt terror over the near certainty he might be killed or permanently maimed by an errant shot. But now, he stood cornered, him or the maiden Zhi Mei. He had no choice of course. Permanently losing face — weighed against death or injury. Like multiple tumblers falling into place for pins of awareness to strike home, his thoughts alighted squarely upon the tapestry of Bao Ling's trap.

It's all about me, he thought. *My spirit roamed unharnessed and worked against itself. Now I get my nose pushed into it. In the form of an arrow delivered by Bao Ling, my own future now subject to darkness and the shift of breezes. And perhaps the sure or unsure hand of the man I had hoped to best.*

He walked up to Bao Ling, speaking only to him, "Anyone ever tell you you're a real firecracker?"

Bao Ling raised his eyebrows, tilting his head, half-acknowledging, then said, "Be kind little brother, after all, you're getting the best viewpoint in the house."

Kong Kong half laughed, now not confident of anything. Only then, with a lighter heart did he cross toward his uncertain fate. *Sometimes I'm just too damned serious about things!*

Bao Ling called out to him. He turned to hear the words, "Don't forget. Hold perfectly still once the arrow is in flight." Bao Ling ended the thought with a wink.

For all but a select few, the shot would have been idiocy. Guan Yu, Zhang Fei, Colonel Sun, Sying Hao, Shi-Hui Ke, more names of comparable skill cannot be readily recalled. Others simply do not have the wherewithal. One's mind controls only so many variables before it unravels and succumbs to chaos and uncertainty, then failure.

Bao Ling set and loaded, taking careful measure of the shot. Kong Kong stood ready, staring intently as the hole in the sovereign appeared, then disappeared while the coin randomly spun, and swung in the now lazy late evening breeze.

Truly, it was the best seat in the house. The young man saw the crowd, feeling their anticipation. The elders stood protectively around poet Zhi Mei. Kuan-Yin looked with concern toward his elder companion. Kong Kong promised the fates that should he survive in one piece, he would take the younger Kuan-Yin under his wing, and together they would partner to grow their talents, so eminently displayed this day.

There, straight away, Bao Ling stood at the ready; he nodded toward Kong Kong. Then he focused on "sung." Relaxing completely, sinking the dantian, rooting, becoming still, listening, then following the dictates of emptiness. His attention tracked the coin and its hollow center, now larger in his mind's eye than the hills beyond. Kong Kong determined he would see the shot on its descent through the hole (heaven willing) to its final end. He lifted the board high.

He smiled, figuring it added to the moment. Bao Ling affirmed in the distance.

Stillness.

Quiet.

Even the lantern flames seemed to freeze.

He saw the bow release, but never saw the arrow. Somewhere in space, a single point raced toward him. Only then did he register the sound of the bow releasing. The sovereign never moved, but the plank exploded in his hands, followed by the roar of the crowd. He felt as though he had fallen from a cliff. In the eternal moment, his old self dropped to the ground, and his spirit lifted free.

Unlike the other, this was no soft shot. The missile exploded from the bow and took the shortest trajectory to its endpoint. For Bao Ling, it was the Yang, to his previously demonstrated Yin. For those in the crowd, eyes chased the arrow, but could not catch its flight. Even the exploding plank surprised them. It seemed the arrow had barely released, was it over already?

Some doubted of course, at least until Master Li Fung, and Abbot Hui secured the sovereign, and took it to the light where traces of charcoal lined its interior, still moist with saliva. As the crowd gathered, they passed the coin, which reverently moved from hand to hand until all had seen, and believed. Only after the last person inspected and stood convinced was the coin returned to Bao Ling.

Kuan-Yin walked to Kong Kong, still standing in the field holding the remnants of the plank, appreciating the unfolding spectacle from afar.

Together they turned and surveyed the scene.

Remembering the aftermath long afterward, Kong Kong one day asked Kuan-Yin, "I saw him lean toward you after the shot. What did he say?"

Kuan-Yin repeated Bao Ling's exact words.

"Now that was a lucky shot!"

An Amazing Shot

Epilogue – The Wizard's Testament

In the cycle of Yin and Yang,
all dogs will have their day.
That includes the mad ones.
Nothing stands permanent.

When the cankered mist of chaos clears.
One gapes to see what caused it to lift.
Little else besides patience, compassion, and dharma.
Oh, and fearlessness of course.
Can't get anywhere without that.

For that reason, it is said.
In life only a handful of freedoms truly exist.
You are free to be compassionate.
You are free to choose action over inertia.
You are free not to be paralyzed or blinded by fear.
You are free to push beyond limitations.

Let those be your banners.

All the rest just gets in the way!

Acknowledgments

Creating a work such as this can be a daunting task. First, the work itself, the endless array of details, the countless re-writes, the editing, the touch ups and fine tuning. Then the layout, now necessitated twice, once for hard copy, once for E-Book. While these processes roll along, life beckons, and insists on our attention. Crises arise, illnesses come and go, surgeries, pandemics, floods, political upheavals, pipes leak, pets get sick and so on to no seeming end. Should I also add the constant stream of pointless texts invading my phone, the tidal waves of memes shooting across my brow, or the rubbish flooding my mail box?

No different than you, I too get sucked into distractions. Luckily, I have one effective counter. Having a dedicated editor … without which nothing would ever arrive at the point of final fruition.

That role has again been voluntarily and unsparingly filled by my friend and fellow explorer of life's mysteries, Bryan Smith. Bryan is a retired professor of mathematics and computer science (Professor Emeritus, University of Puget Sound), who on first learning I was a writer, offered his expert services to edit and opine on anything I planned to publish. Mind you, life's distractions challenge him no less than you or I, so the generosity of his offer speaks clearly to the kindness evident in all Bryan's life undertakings. He's in the dedication for a reason.

Way back when he first offered, I hesitated. I had been down the path before, and often as not, it proved to be an exercise in diversion, if not outright distraction.

But I must say, from the very first, Professor Bryan attacked (I mean that in a positive sense) whatever I tendered with a ruthless, yet fair-minded passion targeting excellence, clarity, polish, and pertinence. In this particular instance, I freely admit for all who will hear. This work has been bettered because of him. Dare I say, even better than had I gone it alone. Thank you Bryan! You have made a profound contribution. To spare you any taint of guilt, I must acknowledge where mistakes and oversights remain, they are all mine. Except the misspellings, those we'll have to share.

Renee Knarreborg once again conjured the artwork you find within. The quality and unique originality speaks for itself. Behind the scenes, I've come to suspect Renee may well be a mind reader. When not tending to regional power and utility issues, or running audits, she somehow finds the time to take in my story lines and character sketches to come up with the final images you see gracing these pages. As I first witness her efforts emerging from the void, I almost feel she has stolen into my subconscious and made real what I could only imagine. As you see, she keeps it simple, often pencil or ink on paper, running through many iterations and exchanges until the images and depictions align, adding an intuitive third dimension to the unfolding tales.

Finally, I am also indebted to the many masters and teachers who have befriended me over the years and who took great care sharing their sagely insights and remarkable skills with this stumbling pilgrim. Most have already passed on, so their work falls to me. To spare any sense of embarrassment, guilt or regret to those remaining, I apologize in advance. None of this is your fault or doing.

About the Author

Billy Ironcrane is the writing and music performing pseudonym for Bill Mc Cabe, a lifelong explorer of life's experiences and unending surprises. Raised in inner city Philadelphia during the 1950's and 60's, he partook in the revolutionary currents of change, protest, activism, and idealism which characterized the era. While a teen, he spent summers on the Jersey coast hawking newspapers, tossing burgers and exploring places like Atlantic City where he encountered flea circuses, Gene Krupa hanging between sets at the Steel Pier, petrified mermaids and the fabulously wealthy promenading the boardwalk at night flashing mink stoles, diamonds, tuxes and studded canes. Atlantic City dubbed itself, "The World's Playground." All the stuff of dreams as he returned to Mrs. J's boarding house where he slept for ten bucks a week, sharing occasional space with his grandfather and other Polish immigrants working the summer trade. Not to mention the landlady's ever present legion of cats.

He departed the inner city still in his teens, and pushed blindly into the unknown never to return. To be static and do nothing would have been terminal, as in fact it proved to be for many of his mates. In the decades following, he pursued new awarenesses, swam exotic currents, wandered remote tropical forests, became a soldier, ambled southwest deserts at night, slept through thunderstorms alongside petrified forests, trekked the Rockies, mastered the martial arts, jogged with blacktail deer in hills surrounding Monterey, explored Zen, motorcycled the California coast, scaled Pfeiffer Rock, freelanced, traversed the Cascades, slept beneath ancient redwoods in remote Los Padres, raised a family, bridged the corporate jungle, then hung a shingle and lived on wits and ingenuity until the muse of the 60's again tapped his shoulder, ordering, "Time to shift gears, Billy."

Characters and Incidentals

Bao Ling - "The Dragon of the Midlands." Protagonist around whom many of our stories revolve. Raised in a remote agrarian community, he opted to resist oppression, taking up arms to defend the weak and helpless. Branded as an outlaw and revolutionary and constantly on the run, he came upon a mysterious stranger, Sying Hao, who offered sanctuary on Southern Mountain. The bargain soon proved to extend far beyond the promised protection. Sying Hao became his mentor, and teacher, honing all of his talents and abilities to their highest realization. In some ways Bao Ling is everyman … just trying to make sense of the unknowable and the uncertain, while preserving his connections to the simple life of his forbears, and to the land and people he loves.

Cao Cao - (155 - 15 March 220 CE). King of and then posthumously declared Emperor of Wei. Ambitious and talented general who sought to harness the Will of Heaven and establish a new empire in place of the failed Han. A talented leader, warrior, strategist, and scholar, as well as a renowned poet. Universally regarded as ruthless, cruel and merciless in securing his objectives, but grudgingly acknowledged for love of family and remarkable loyalty to friends and allies. History tells how he succeeded to a considerable degree. His piece of empire is remembered as the "Cao Wei." This should not be confused with lesser successors, also named Wei. All mere shadows of the original. What he forged lasted less than half a century. Hardly a blip in the roll of dynasties. His doings unfolded long before the events of our stories, but lingered as factors nonetheless. What remained after his demise were many conflicting ambitions driving lesser personalities to propel the great land deeper into chaos. Pervasive suffering beset the masses. Generations came and went with no promise of any ending. The warring kingdoms alluded to in our accounts were mere shadows of the original "Cao Wei." No more than specters of what once was. Except in the degree of violence and torment which they wrought vying for control of everything. Forever, they scrounged every which way to replenish resources depleted by interminable waves of war machines foolishly unleashed. All quite real and unprecedented. Therein lies the significance and relevance of once forgotten places like Ling village and the Shu mountain passes. Perhaps they might prove to be the difference.

Cao Pi - Son and successor to Cao Cao. Forced the Emperor Xian to abdicate, sealing the demise of Han. Also a renowned poet.

Cao Zhi - Lost the succession of Cao Cao to his more politically astute brother Cao Pi. Managed to have his life spared by meeting two impossible poetry challenges issued by his brother Cao Pi. He spent the balance of his life barred from court and courtly influence. But for his poetry, he would likely have disappeared from history.

Colonel Sun (Sun Wu Kong) - Honored officer and counselor in the service of Liu Bei. Close comrade to Zhuge Liang and colleague to Guan Yu. Mentor and fatherly influence to Sying Hao. Possibly an immortal, possibly a descendant of a different species. Forever shrouded in mystery. In no small part due to his guarded and reticent demeanor, barely offsetting his forboding and ever solemn presence. His life and deeds linger as monuments preserved in legend and enshrined as myth. Directly, or indirectly, his influence and spirit can be felt throughout our tales, and seem to ripple through the ages. We speak of him at considerable length over the course of many accounts and recollections.

Deshi Ku - "The ancient one." One of the mountain people. Esteemed tribal elder and regarded as chieftain. A healer and facilitator revered for his knowledge, and his life connection to heroes of the past.

Dishi Jou - Mountain People. A village elder. The one who watched the waters, and managed their improbable flows with consummate skill.

Fortune's Gateway - A major trade center on the western end of the Shu mountain ranges, backed by the great western wilderness, an endless expanse, and what remained of the defunct Silk Road which had long before proven so beneficial to the Han Dynasty. Despite the collapse of Han, and afterward, the collapse of the Shu Han (the western empire headed by Liu Bei), Fortune's Gateway proved very much to be deserving of its name. There, one found a lineage of traders who prospered by treating all parties as equals, so long as they had something to transact, and needed something in return. Foremost among those parties were the Shu people of the mountains, long oppressed, and forever contending with invaders from the east. Being practical, many in Fortune's Gateway recognized the continuing benefit of their association with the Shu. So long as the mountain tribes fended off those in the east, Fortune's Gateway remained for all practical purposes autonomous. They had once flourished under Liu Bei, and even within the time frame of this account largely remained insulated from upheavals in the east, thanks to the resistance of the Shu mountain tribes.

Guanyin - Bodhisattva of compassion, somehow connected in essence to Zhi Mei.

Guan Yu - (160-220 CE). Also referred to as Guan Gong (Lord Guan), or simply Guan. Sworn brother to Liu Bei and Zhang Fei (bound three as one by their Peach Garden Oath). Virtually peerless among human warriors. Revered as a staunch patron of righteousness. Protector of the oppressed, guardian of the weak and vulnerable. Particularly the Shu tribes, in whom he took an unshakable personal interest. In the lineage of our accounts, he becomes companion and peer to Sun Wu Kong (Colonel Sun). He is the only human ever considered by Sun Wu Kong to be his martial equal. In his prime, with no more than his Green Dragon Blade in hand, Guan Yu could alone, stand down an entire enemy army.

He Ling - Paternal Grandfather to Bao Ling. Of considerable influence in shaping his character and developing his unique talents. Though little is said of him in this account, in time he will be shown connected to a history of mysterious influences which only become apparent to Bao Ling as his own journey into uncertainty and challenge continues.

Hung (Red Faced Liu) - Hung Lian Liu; mountain tribe archer of legend.

Iron Hand Gao - Friend of He Ling. Martial and life tutor to the child Bao Ling. He is mentioned only in a passing reference. Though their time together had been short due to harsh necessity, the impact of his character on Bao Ling had been profound. After encountering a man like Iron Hand Gao, one is unlikely to fear any other.

Jin Dynasty - (265-420 CE). War of the Eight Princes. The period leading up to and enveloping our stories.

Kong Kong - Mountain People. Threw the brazen challenge to Bao Ling which resulted in the archery contest. The village elders are fearful the talented young warrior's unbridled need for reward and acclaim may lead to his ruin.

Kuan-Yin Ting - Mountain People. Orphaned mountain herder who first encounters Bao Ling while minding livestock for Shu-Ting tribe. In short order, he becomes friend and disciple to Bao Ling. Though nearly opposite in personal nature to the brash Kong Kong ... the two soon enough recognize the ascending skills and character, each in the other.

Li Fung - "Master Li" of the Mountain People. Village elder. Martial master. He figures prominently in the personal development of Shi-Hui Ke, both as child, and as man. In our book *Seed of Dragons*, we give full account of the man and the considerable influence he has over his people. Now he is older. His one time protege, Shi-Hui Ke, stands nearly his equal in the high esteem of the mountain tribes.

Li Kong - Mountain People. Village elder and master of physical laws. Renowned bridge maker.

Liu Bei - (unknown 161 – 10 June 223 CE). The incomparable man of righteousness. A common man, though distant relation to the Han emperor. A sandal maker who rose to prominence as a formidable military commander — driven by his unsparing dedication to restoration of the Han Dynasty. Retreating to save what remained of his forces, he founded the Shu Han empire in the remote west, and prospered beyond all expectations — his achievements the stuff of dreams and legends. Until his demise, he remained a key principal during the period of the Three Kingdoms. He felt the Shu tribes to be a most noble and honorable people, believing that so long as they remained viable, there would be no direct path for Cao Cao and Wei to attack from the east. To that end, he ensured the Shu remained independent, and always, a respected ally. He nurtured, encouraged, and taught them how to fend for themselves.

Man From Southern Mountain - A mysterious mystic and teacher of legendary renown. Some would argue him to be one and the same as Jiang Ziya, others say the same of Sying Hao. At the time of our telling, the matter has not been settled.

Peach Garden Oath - Three young men meet in fate, and find themselves of common heart. They agree to bind their destinies to hopes for a just and prosperous land. Liu Bei, Guan Yu and Zhang Fei swear to be as brothers in united purpose. Avenge the Han, restore the nation, bring peace, exercise compassion to the helpless and needy. Liu Bei as eldest, becomes leader. Guan Yu his second. Though not born on the same day, by their oath they commit themselves unto death, memorialized in their expressed hope to die on the same day, in the same month and year. They call upon the immortals to seal their pact, and to strike dead whosoever fails its purpose or betrays their sworn fraternity. The actual oath can be found in Chapter One of *Romance of the Three Kingdoms* by the 14th century playwright Luo Guanzhong.

Shi-Hui Ke - One of the Shu Mountain people. Abbot of Crystal Springs temple, a mysterious preserve and one of several fortresses meticulously conceived by Zhuge Liang to secure the Shu Roads from invasion. Created, in accordance with Liu Bei's directive, to protect and preserve the culture and heritage of the mountain people. Although a monk and man of peace, Shi-Hui Ke remains an ardent patriot, and has found purpose in his role as defender of his people and their ways. In his youth, he had attained renown as a singularly gifted martial artist, particularly in archery, before losing his left arm midway from the shoulder resulting from unlucky encounter with a sadistic band of Wei mercenaries. They removed his left thumb, assuring he could wield no bow. Gangrene set in and the arm could not be saved. In some ways, the unfortunate loss of his arm proved a blessing ... in time, the once consummate archer, now monk, found within his higher states of awareness, the secret of the "thought arrow." Bao Ling had opportunity to witness Abbot Hui's remarkable skill, projecting nothing but concentrated thought to strike and deter a stalking tiger. The full account is presented herein. He also appears to have gained privy to the alchemy of longevity, or so concludes Bao Ling, but that's a different story.

Shu-Ting tribe - The displaced mountain people residing in the environs surrounding Crystal Springs. A collection of displaced castaways, looking to reform and restore their culture. This branch of the Shu has a long history of dealings with those in Fortune's Gateway. Over time, the two groups have become respectfully interdependent.

Sying Hao - Mentor to Bao Ling. A onetime war orphan who became apprentice and adopted son to Sun Wu Kong. Friend of the Southlanders and archer supreme. Scholar of the classics, and bow craftsman of singular caliber. Guided by Sun, he mastered the transformations, learned to project consciousness, and to move about undetected. Thought by many to be a ghost. Sometimes called "Fenghua Yan" (weathered rock), or "The Man from Southern Mountain."

The Five Tiger Generals - The five generals who served Liu Bei with uncompromising loyalty throughout his reign. Many times, their valor and exemplary leadership proved decisive against what others deemed insurmountable odds. By Lord Liu's designation they were:

Guan Yu - General of the Front;
Zhang Fei - General of the Right;
Huang Zhong - General of the Rear;

Ma Chao - General of the Left; and
Zhao Yun - General of the Center.

History honors them as "The Five Tiger Generals."

Yama - "King Yama." A devil of sorts, or perhaps what we might think of as the incarnation of death. Presides over hell and is accountable for the life, death and transmigration of human souls. Keeps true the final ledger and ensures his fearsome legions bring the newly departed to their end judgment. Relishes chaos and induces strife. Truly enjoys his job, particularly the part where he gets to torment those deserving. Once, when confronted by the Creator for his evil doings, he defended himself most eloquently, arguing to the Creator, "Hey ... isn't this my job? Did you make me for any other purpose? Can you think of anyone who can do it better than me? Forgive me sire, but I fail to see where there is a problem." Convinced by his logic and impressed with his integrity, the Creator ordered his release declaring him free to go about his business unimpeded.

Zhang Fei - (unknown - died 221 CE). Sworn brother to Guan Yu and Liu Bei. Also a singular warrior, one whom Guan Yu deemed his peer and often boasted of. Known for his uncontrollable temper, it proved to be his ultimate undoing, said to have been assassinated by his own men. But not until fulfilling a life of epic feats and undeniable heroism.

Zhao Yun - One of the illustrious five generals serving Liu Bei throughout his lifetime, and beyond. Zhao Yun passed in 229 CE. His day of birth is unknown but most believe him 60 years old at the time of his death. He dedicated his entire life and lived above all things to serve the cause of Liu Bei and the Shu Han. In our prior work, *Token Tales and Fragments*, we allude to the possibility his direct blood line includes Bao Ling.

Many remembrances of his deeds echo within *Romance of the Three Kingdoms*. Typically, they recall his supreme martial skill, unbounded courage, penetrating intellect, as well as the loyalty and admiration of those who served with and under him. To the present, his high principles and righteous character remain common knowledge throughout the land, modeling standards revered by all.

Even today, in Henan Province he may sometimes appear as entrance deity, along with his comrade Ma Chao, together protecting Taoist temples from the influence of evil spirits.

Zhi Mei - A farm girl whose family (father and brother) were killed by Wei marauders. She had been kidnapped and abused until stumbled upon and rescued by Bao Ling. Alone and vulnerable, she accepts Bao Ling's offer to partner as traveling companions to Crystal Springs. She comes from a family of skilled poets, and though a common farm girl, possesses consummate skill in rhyme and song. In time, her words become the voice of the resistance, and her accounts and stories record the noble deeds of its heroes, particularly the Dragon of the Midlands.

Zhuge Liang (181 - 234 CE) - Sometimes referred to as "Kongming" the Sleeping Dragon, attesting to the splendor of his essential nature once unleashed. A wizard, scholar, musician and hero whose influence and guiding hand

threads either directly or indirectly throughout our accounts,
and perhaps beyond them. Despite his many deeds of
record, historical records say little of his past, or his
background. No one can account for how he gained his
remarkable talents. For that reason, he remains an enigma.
In our recitations, the dates of his life are indeterminate. He
has achieved longevity; though, not having fully mastered
its alchemy, he is not a true immortal. As a Merlin like sage
who has perfected awareness, he stands singular, and
among humans and other creatures, is spoken of in the same
breath and with the same reverence as only the likes of Jiang
Ziya and Sun Wu Kong.

Other Works by Billy Ironcrane

Returning to Center
(A Collection of Stories, Vignettes and Thoughts)
2018

Seed of Dragons
(Surviving an Empire Undone)
2019

Token Tales and Fragments
(Recalling a Time of Heroes and Sages)
2020

Made in the USA
Middletown, DE
24 November 2021

52860652R00179